MENNONITES

DON'T

DANCE

MENNONITES DON'T DANCE

❦

DARCIE FRIESEN HOSSACK

thistledown press

Thistledown Press Ltd.
633 Main Street
Saskatoon, Saskatchewan, S7H 0J8
www.thistledownpress.com

Library and Archives Canada Cataloguing in Publication

Cover photograph, *The Suicide*, by Madalina Iordache-Levay
Cover and book design by Jackie Forrie
Printed and bound in Canada

Mixed Sources
Cert no. SW-COC-001271
© 1996 FSC
FSC

Canada Council   Conseil des Arts   SASKATCHEWAN   ∎♦∎   Canadian   Patrimoine
for the Arts   du Canada   ARTS BOARD   Heritage   canadien

Thistledown Press gratefully acknowledges the financial assistance of the Canada Council for the Arts, the Saskatchewan Arts Board, and the Government of Canada through the Canada Book Fund for its publishing program.

MENNONITES
DON'T
DANCE

To Dean,
for wearing an "I Love My Wife" T-shirt and meaning it

and Daphne,
for bringing the broom and dustpan.

Contents

Luna

IN THE WINTER THAT JONAH TURNED twelve, his favourite uncle died.

By all measures Elias Froese, a farmer who also built barns by trade, was a healthy, strong ox of a man. Tall, temperate. A Samson, people said. Jonah and his friends sometimes tried to perform chin-ups from his outstretched arms.

"The man's not afraid of hard work, that's certain," other people said about Elias, usually to Jonah's father, who quietly absorbed the compliment to his brother like a blow to his gut. When he got home, he'd put a hole in the wall, which Jonah patched from a bucket of plaster. Later though, his father might apologize.

"Your uncle's a better man than me, son. No sense my feeling sore over what the Lord saw fit to make. There's a lesson in that."

Jonah didn't know whether the lesson was supposed to be that God was unfair, or some people were meant to aspire to what others already came by naturally. Or, that one good man in a family could cancel out the bad in another.

It seemed to Jonah that the people from their village believed they were each somehow responsible for Elias being such a fine man. They congratulated themselves. But Jonah didn't think it had anything to do with them. If so, his father, from the same village, would be the same kind of person. And his heart wouldn't have hardened so completely after Elias died and and he no longer had his brother to compare himself to.

Years later, what people still remembered about Elias was that at the end of each day of work he would stand quietly, raise his hands up over his head and lift his face to the sky. The harder the job, the higher he'd lift his face. As though his sweat was being exchanged for jewels in his heavenly crown. Although many thought it an unnecessary display — too showy for their liking — very few spoke out against it. Some thought he had earned every ruby he could take from the hand of God, and hoped some would spill over onto them. Others would try to pay him a couple more pennies for his work than they'd agreed on, purchasing second-hand notice from heaven. Jonah knew that the extra money always ended up in the offering plate on Sunday.

When Elias became sick, people wondered what sins he might have committed and wished they had those pennies back in their own pockets. They began to ask among themselves whether Jonah's father, with his grim posture in church, who had quietly suffered years of meagre crops even when those around his had thrived, had somehow done more than Elias to earn God's favour. After all, Elias had been taken and Abram had not.

Elias's illness started with an ache and a chill that seemed like the flu. Jonah noticed that his uncle's breath smelled fecal. His face became ashen. It slackened like soft clay sliding off his bones. Within a week, he stopped work on the barn he was building for the Martins' family. The Martins lived two miles to the south and were known, according to Jonah's father — who had borrowed money from them once — as being unforgiving of debts.

Elias assured them he'd be back to work just as soon as he had his strength back. After a month passed, and another, even the old country doctor had to accept what no one in the community wanted to believe. It wouldn't be long before Elias was in the ground, and it didn't seem that God had any interest in dispensing a miracle.

Jonah saw that his uncle was alone in being at peace about his death. Elias told him that his days were measured out before the beginning of the world, and that would do just fine for him. As for the few earthly things he would leave behind, they were for Jonah.

"The house will be closed up and the crops will be your dad's until your twentieth birthday. Then the land is yours. Just remember that it belongs to the Lord first, and it will always be blessed."

When Elias finally died, those who knew him agreed it was a shame that such a big man should wither up like he had. The undertaker remarked that he had put Elias in a coffin that was two sizes smaller than if he'd simply fallen off a roof. He seemed to regret that Elias was denied the spectacle of an over-large coffin. As it was, when mourners came for a last look at his body, Elias appeared ordinary in a diminished sort of way. The same as anyone who had died that sort of death.

After the funeral, Jonah's father appeared more angry at Mrs. Martins than sad about Elias. He said the woman had cornered him at the back of the church and made sure to complain that Elias could have at least finished their barn before he went and got sick. "Says it's December and she has no place for her stinking cows except to rent stalls for the buggers in a neighbour's barn. Had the nerve to suggest Elias hadn't looked all that bad to her for the first few weeks and it might've done him some good to keep busy. Bloody coffin was right there and the woman still couldn't hold her tongue."

"She said that?" said Jonah's mother, one of the few times Jonah heard her question his father.

"Well, she may as well have said it as much as thought it."

Jonah felt sorry that the Martins were that sort of people when, to him, they showed every appearance of being just the opposite. He had a hard time imagining Mrs. Martins saying anything unkind. But he supposed that it meant she must be two-faced, which was the worst way to be.

After the funeral was the only time Jonah ever saw his father cry. When everyone else had left, he sat in a pew and bawled like a woman. His body, folded over his lap, shook so violently that Jonah thought the grief would unhook his father's spine. Once his tears were wrung out, he drove them home in their rusted Ford pickup, cursing God in a continuous stream that Jonah and his mother didn't dare interrupt. He swore and said that if God didn't make exceptions for a man like his brother — a good man people loved — he himself was as good as dead. Like others, Jonah's father believed that he lived on grace borrowed from Elias.

At home, he became quiet, his silence a crust growing over a wound.

"That woman," Jonah's father finally said after three solid days of silence, the word woman spat out like a bitter taste. "How dare she talk to me like that? As though Elias deserved what he got because her rutting cattle have to shit in someone else's barn for a season. I suppose she thinks it's up to me now, but she's got a long time to sit on her fat ass if she's waiting for me to darken her doorstep."

The next morning, an hour before the sun was up, Jonah woke to a single sharp blow to his bedroom door. He sat up straight and threw off his blanket.

"Let's go," his father said, striking the door hard a second time. Without opening it to ask where or why, Jonah piled on his clothes. He hurried outside and picked up a heavy metal box of tools that his father pointed to, lying on the frost-covered path in front of the house. They walked, crunching over gravel and snow, Jonah behind by a few steps as he struggled with the awkward weight of his burden and shifted it from hand to hand.

"Too much for you?" Jonah's father said without looking back. It felt like an accusation, but Jonah reasoned that his father just needed time to come to terms with his loss. Before, when something had caused him to fall into one of his moods, he always struggled back to the surface for a while.

"I'm fine," Jonah said, though his fingers were stiff and his lungs felt brittle with cold, making him desperate to stop and indulge in a fit of coughing.

"Good, because tomorrow you can get up early and do your chores before we go. Had to do the milking myself this morning."

Jonah, to keep from falling farther behind, held his breath and ran to catch up, the toolbox throwing him off balance. He didn't drop back again and they arrived at the Martins' farm just as the sun was beginning to show. Mr. Martins was coming out of the house with a slop pail full of plate scrapings, grapefruit peels, and egg shells for his pigs. He stopped and considered Jonah and his father.

"Can't say I know what's brought you here, Abram," he said. He gently set down the pail and the wire handle fell and chimed against the side. It felt to Jonah like an invitation to do the same, to put the toolbox by his feet, but he didn't think he could let go. His fingers were stiff as though they had frozen around the handle.

"Come to do a bit of unfinished business, is all," Jonah's father said after a few moments, which, to Jonah, seemed eternal.

"Not your responsibility, as I see it, but you're welcome if it's what you want." Mr. Martins looked from Jonah's father to Jonah to the unfinished barn, its undressed frame salted with beads of snow.

For a week after that, except on Sunday, Jonah got up and was busy with the milking before his father's feet hit the floor. It was still dark when he finished and even the cows seemed to know it was too early to protest with their usual fidgeting and swishes of their manure-crusted tails. When he was done, Jonah waited in the barn where it was warm enough to keep from shivering. As soon as he heard his father's feet on the gravel outside, Jonah snatched up the toolbox — his father said he didn't trust leaving it with the Martins — and was ready to walk.

Working together, Jonah and his father finished sooner than they expected, and Jonah felt satisfied to have completed his uncle's work. Pleased, too, he had done something measurable to help his father and mother. The money from the job would be useful, he was sure. Maybe they'd even celebrate by killing a chicken for supper that night.

At the Martins' door, Jonah stepped forward and knocked before retreating to stand just behind his father. Every day after they finished, Mrs. Martins had invited them in to warm up with a cup of coffee, a slice of fresh pie, or a share of whatever baking she had done during the afternoon. Every day Jonah's father refused.

"I guess we're done here," Jonah's father said when Mrs. Martins opened the door. Jonah could smell fresh bread and imagined eating it with a thick slab of butter and a spoonful of jam. He thought his father must be wrong about her and believed that this time, because they were finished, because she was so kind, his father would accept her invitation.

"Come on in," said Mrs. Martins. "Get yourselves out of the cold." She opened the door wider and warm, yeasty air flowed over Jonah's face, leaving it moist, then colder than before.

"No, I don't think so. We'll just be on our way." It had happened the same way each day, but Jonah still felt that this time would have to be different. Surely his father wouldn't keep them standing in the cold while Mrs. Martins went inside for the money.

"At least come in while I fetch you your envelope," she said. Jonah took an involuntary step towards her, but took it back when his father didn't move.

"I won't accept that," Jonah's father said. "It's not rightfully mine. It belongs to Elias and he's not here to take it." He doffed his hat, a grey felt fedora, and turned round, leaving Jonah still looking at Mrs. Martins. He swallowed hard, as though a sharp stone had lodged in his throat. He was unable to tear his eyes from her until she reached back inside the house. Mrs. Martins opened the envelope and pressed a warm dollar into Jonah's hand, squeezing it in both of hers, and closed the door.

"Miserable old sow'd be sure to remind me and everyone else about her bleedin' barn until Kingdom come," Jonah's father said after they were half a mile down the road. "Didn't deserve what we did for them."

Jonah nodded as though he understood. A little while later, Jonah's father took the toolbox from him and carried it the rest of the way. But without the weight he'd become accustomed to it was hard for Jonah to walk straight.

"You know that disease of your uncle's runs in families," Jonah's father said as they walked. Ever since Elias died, he'd been unable to speak the disease's name. As though it would invite the cancer in. "Means my number's up next, and you should go ahead and plan to get done what you want to get done long before you're my age. All a man can do is work hard enough, and take as little as he needs, so that the Old Bastard upstairs doesn't take notice. Then just go on and die as well as you can."

That night, Jonah didn't sleep. He sat on his bed, uncomfortably awake, wrapped in a rough quilt that smelled of wet wool from his own cold sweat. He turned over in his mind what his father had said about hard work and reward, until he looked at it from all sides, until he believed it.

When Jonah finally lay down, he held his breath and stayed as still as he could. Thoughts of stuff going wrong inside him swooped down, veering away at the last second before he was able to catch and reason with them. He began to shiver. It wasn't until morning, when the sun glared past the edges of the heavy brocade drapes over his window, that he thought of looking for an extra, dry blanket.

Jonah dressed before his parents were up. Although it was a warmer day than those before, Jonah ached from a chill that had seeped under his skin and into his bones. He felt starved, full of holes, but had no appetite. Without breakfast, he completed his morning chores. When finished, he set off to clean the old outhouse, a weather-worn shamble of sticks his mother had lately complained wasn't fit to be used.

For an hour, Jonah scrubbed frozen fly specks from the walls and seat, swept up the bodies of insects that had died in the fall — the flies that spun on their backs until they finally succumbed, the moths that had shed the ability to eat along with their soft caterpillar bodies. He poured lye down the toilet hole and could have finished there; it would have been enough. If it were spring, he would have searched in the dark corners and between the boards for spiders — daddy-longlegs, mostly — even though they ate mosquitoes. He would have crushed them with his thumb, each one popping like a blister. Instead, he whisked away their crumbling webs and brushed them off onto his pants. By the last web, his hands were gloved in grimy spider silk.

When he was through, Jonah walked around the outhouse, and walked around it again, worrying tracks down to the frozen dirt under the snow. It was still filthy, he thought, disappointed in a way he couldn't understand. He crouched down on his heels, bowed his head under his hands and cringed at what he felt he needed to do. He thought about the boys his age that he knew were going pond skating that afternoon, maybe playing hockey if there were enough of them. For a moment, he closed his eyes and imagined the ice under his blades, the feeling of freedom. He shook his head, driving away the image.

With extra lumber that he and his father had gone back and hauled away after finishing the Martins' barn — his father said it rightfully belonged to Elias and wouldn't leave it there — Jonah began to work on building a new outhouse. He sawed and hammered wood together into a frame, sawdust and the occasional drop of blood staining the trampled snow under his feet. When the frame was up, he dressed it with plumb horizontal slats. On the inside he sanded any wood that might be touched when someone visited. He worked without rest, without water, his breath shallow and tight, as though sucking air through a paper straw. Finally, he picked up an axe and began to chop a new hole in the frozen ground. When it was deep enough, he pushed and dragged the new outhouse over top. Against the side he piled firewood, having heard that women, if there were men nearby when they came to do their business, preferred to maintain their dignity and instead carry off a few sticks for the stove. Although he couldn't believe his mother really cared either way. She was too busy trying to anticipate her husband's temper, aware of every time he looked her up and down and scowled, every time he fingered a piece of furniture and rubbed the dust between his fingers. Or sloshed stew back and forth in his bowl, trying to see whether there was anything worth eating underneath the watery surface.

Jonah stood and arched his back, muscles tightly bundled from bending over his work. In the time since he'd started, a storm front had pushed its way down from the north. Jonah could see it gaining on the horizon, feeding on the warmer air that had briefly settled over the prairie. And while he knew the storm could shift to the east and leave them be, it was a better bet to put on an extra layer of clothing and be ready for the cold.

The last thing Jonah did before the storm came was go into the old outhouse and throw the dollar Mrs. Martins had given him into the hole.

One day, late the following summer, while Jonah oiled the gravel driveway to keep down the dust, his father came outside and stopped him. He put his hand on Jonah's shoulder and exhaled, a resigned, coarse sound. Someone else might have thought he was angry, but Jonah leaned towards it as though it was a blessing.

"I'm sorry, son. It's not fair to you that your dad's such an old shit," he said.

Jonah's heart, which had swelled a moment before, shrunk back.

"I don't think — " Jonah said, but his father interrupted him.

"Don't need you to lie to me," he said. "I know what I am. People are all a waste. You know that, don't you? The world'd be better off without us in it. See these grasshoppers?" He deliberately crushed a few insects with the toe of his worn-out boot. "We're more like them than we are those crows over there — at least they serve some use, cleaning up after what dies. A plague, that's what people are." He patted Jonah on the back, sadly, as though they had reached another understanding.

After that Jonah often left his suppers half-eaten on his plate, telling his mother he didn't need more than his share. There was no room in his stomach. He had swallowed the seed of what his father said and it began to put out roots.

Three years later, when Jonah was fifteen, a letter arrived in the mail from his Aunt Ardelle, his mother's sister who lived on a farm near Brandon in Manitoba, several hours northeast of Swift

Current by train. Shortly after, Jonah was sent to live with her for the summer.

"She just needs a little help keeping up, is all," was how Jonah's mother put it. He could tell her mouth was full of words that wanted to spill out. "Your father and I agree it's a good idea," she added, before swallowing the rest.

She avoided looking at him as she gave him the news — folding bleach-ravaged laundry into haphazard piles as she spoke — and he knew that he was being sent away. He knew, too, that it was his father who wanted him to go, even if he never said so himself. Lately he had begun to look at Jonah as though he were a debt, a reminder that he owed more to God than he had. Seeing this, Jonah's mother had thought of a way to borrow a cup of grace.

"Your father just needs some time," Jonah's mother said. They were already at the train platform in Swift Current, and he had asked her whether it wasn't more important that he stay home and help with the farm.

"Your father feels so responsible for us," she said. "He'll be better after a few months with less to think about. And you'll like your aunt. She's always had a soft spot for children and wasn't married long enough to have her own before her husband died. He had insurance." Jonah's mother looked away from him, to the open door of the train car. "She just keeps a few chickens for the extra money." She picked up Jonah's bag, handed it to him and walked away without looking back. Minutes later, the train's engine coughed a plume of black smoke and lurched forward, before easing into the straight row of tracks and gaining speed.

Jonah thought about his mother and Aunt Ardelle most of the way to Brandon, and decided there was no other possible way for his aunt to be other than thick in the middle and the ankles. When she'd wear one of her spongy polyester dresses — which his mother wore like a uniform — she would look as though she was upholstered. Like a chesterfield whose stuffing had shifted.

So when an evenly plump and merry-looking woman in a sensible but flower-printed cotton dress came towards him at the train station, he didn't know it was Ardelle until she clasped her hands and called out his name. Still, he thought it must be a mistake.

"Well, aren't you just the image of your old dad?" She laughed as she pulled him into a hearty embrace that smelled of cream gravy and farmer's sausage. "No matter, though," she said, taking Jonah by the shoulders to have a better look. "Nothing's fixed until you're in the ground. And I've got you for a summer to myself. No telling what we can do with you in that time."

The room Jonah's aunt had prepared for him was white and cool with crisp, light linens and goose-down pillows on a narrow, plush bed. There was a soft rag rug on the floor. The air smelled of line-dried laundry. Sunshine, but not the way he thought of it at home. At home, when the sun seeped in through his mother's curtains, it was the colour of urine, dry as dust.

Jonah sat on the edge of a chair arranged under the window and wondered what to do next. Ardelle had instructed him to rest until she called him for supper. "Have a little lie-down until you get your land legs back underneath you." Jonah had to admit that it was a good idea. He felt a little strange, as though the ground were still moving under his feet and his body swaying slightly from side to side like the train.

With nothing to distract him, Jonah had time to consider how he must look to his aunt.

Even though every stitch his mother had sent him in was painstakingly clean, he was self-conscious of his trousers, which were thinning at the knees and left too many inches of sock showing below the hem. He had grown in the last year, and it wasn't that his parents couldn't afford the few things that were most needed. It was that his father saw no point. Jonah would just grow out of the next pair of pants, too.

At supper, Jonah was hungrier than he could ever remember. Although he'd done nothing but sit the whole day, his stomach felt deep and unfillable, as though it had expanded since the last time he ate.

"Didn't ask your mother what you like, so I've made a bit of everything." Ardelle put down the dish she'd been carrying and lifted the lid, letting a cloud of steam rise into the air. "The baby potatoes with cream and dill's my favourite, if you want to know. New potatoes from the garden, just this morning. My husband used to say that if you put them next to some of that roast beef or the farmer's sausage, no man'd ever want to leave my kitchen."

Jonah was unsure whether he should say something consoling, or something complimentary about the food. Or both.

"I'm sure he was right," he said, hoping it was appropriate.

"He usually was, except for when he wasn't," Ardelle said, laughing. Jonah pinched his lips together and bit them. It wasn't his place to joke.

Jonah took small helpings of the potatoes and beef, which Ardelle quickly doubled. After that, she passed him one casserole dish after another. It didn't seem right to refuse and, by the last dish, the fullness of his plate made him blush.

"That's cassoulet," Ardelle said when Jonah tapped a spoonful of something with green beans onto his plate. "I'm known for it when we old church ladies have a potluck. Silly old ducks, most of them. The Lord and I know half of them could use a stiff shot of vanilla now and again."

In bed that night, surrounded by fresh linens, Jonah thought about home. His mother would be snoring, seeming to sleep as fast as she could to make up for how little time there was before breakfast, chores. His father, beside her, always lay flat on his back with his arms at his side, dead silent. When Jonah was little, he used to creep into their room to watch for the rise and fall of his father's chest, before sneaking back to his own bed. Until now, he had never slept anywhere else.

During the days at his aunt's, there was barely enough work for Jonah to keep himself busy, and Ardelle seldom asked him to do anything specific. He spent his first weeks with her looking for extra chores that needed doing. Ardelle was unfussy but efficient, and paid a pair of young neighbour boys to help her with things she couldn't manage. Early in the mornings Jonah went with her to collect eggs from the henhouse, reached under the bellies of hens. They walked from house to house in the village to sell the eggs. He had a feeling though, that he was just along for a little fresh air and exercise. That, and Ardelle seemed to enjoy introducing him.

"Here, you can take this out to the barn," she said one morning when Jonah came into the kitchen, still muzzy with having overslept. She was cracking and whisking the last of the day-old eggs into a pail of fresh, warm milk. The pail was only half full; the rest Ardelle had poured off into bottles.

"You don't have cows," he said, peering into the pail of milk with its swirls of bright yellow yolk.

"No, but the neighbours do," Ardelle said in a teasing way. "Now, there are three tin dishes right where you first go into the barn. Pour milk in all of them, but more in the one with the red rim. Wait until they're done, then bring me back the pail and the dishes to wash." She handed him three stale buns and instructed him to break them into pieces and pour the yolky milk over top.

Outside, the morning light was thin and grey, as though it had been steeped with Earl Grey tea, obscuring the outbuildings across the yard. Jonah could tell that the day would be warm, although there was a lightness in the air that he hadn't noticed before. The milk sloshed slightly in the pail. He had carried thousands of pails of milk in his fifteen years, but never any of them fortified with eggs. Of course the strange combination must be for his aunt's cats. Since arriving, Jonah had seen them around her property — black and white ones, mostly, with glossy fur that reminded him of men's church shoes. Back home any cats without enough sense to find someone else's barn were expected to fend for themselves. They were dull and tatty about the ears, with inflamed, mucousy eyes and sometimes bent tails that had been broken under the foot of a cow. In their hayloft Jonah sometimes found emaciated kittens, half-eaten by their mothers.

A few of his aunt's cats, ones that waited expectantly at the door to the house every morning, stood up, stretched and followed Jonah to the barn. They wound around his legs and made throaty, purring meowing sounds when he stopped to lift the pitted iron latch and open the wooden door, its grain dry and split by weather and age. On the other side there were more cats and kittens — Jonah counted thirty-one in all, including an enormous feathery-furred tom, which presided over the red-rimmed dish. The rest sat around the other dishes, as though they were diners waiting to be served.

"We had a dog for a while," Jonah said one morning when he'd been with his aunt for more than a month. Ardelle looked up from the pot of oatmeal she was stirring and he saw that she quickly hid a look of surprise.

"A dog," she repeated. A nudge to go on.

"A little one, I don't know what kind it was. A Heinz 57, I guess. I remember once, we were having sausages for supper. She wanted one something terrible, but Dad had taught her to sit still or get walloped."

Ardelle put her pot to the back of the stove and turned to give him her full attention. She seemed to sense that Jonah was about to falter.

"Anyway." Jonah swallowed. "I could see that she was trying to get close, but she was moving so slow that Dad didn't see her until she was all the way to the table. She jumped up and snatched the sausage from his plate and ran off. Dad got up and they chased each other around and around the table with him calling 'Get back here, you little *schweinhund*, you little sausage snatcher!'"

Ardelle, who had lightly clamped a hand over her mouth until that moment, suddenly laughed out loud. A big, delighted bark of a sound that sent her teeth skittering across the kitchen floor. Jonah forgot about being nervous and watched the teeth in surprise, then looked at his aunt, her mouth round and open and empty. Seeing the look on her face, he burst into laughter and they howled together until his back ached and his eyes spilled over with tears.

"Too much sugar when I was a girl," Ardelle said when they finally recovered enough and she bent to fetch her dentures, rinse and pop them back in her mouth. "Your mom's still got all of hers. Probably she'll be buried with every one of her original teeth still in her head."

"She lost one last winter," Jonah said. He looked down and away, unsure of himself.

"Did she now?"

"Yeah," Jonah said. "She fell on some ice and it broke. A front one, too. After that it turned all black and she had to have it pulled."

"Well, it's nothing to laugh at, though it'll do." Ardelle grinned at Jonah until he couldn't help but do the same. Later he wondered why he had told her that about the dog, his mother's tooth.

At the end of summer, Ardelle drove Jonah back to the train in Brandon. Already the trees were beginning to turn gold and red around the edges. There was a chill in the air, a current underneath the lingering warmth of the season. Together at the station, Jonah and Ardelle sat on a bench and waited. For a while neither of them said anything until she handed Jonah a lunch box filled with a jar of milk, four beef and mashed potato sandwiches, and a slab of lemon squares to eat on his trip back home.

"It doesn't mean you don't love your parents if you choose to believe in a little grace." Into his hand Ardelle pressed a leaf of thin India paper that he recognized as having been torn from a Bible. On it a verse was circled, which she told him to remember for a time when he might need it. *For I know the plans I have for you, declares the Lord, plans to prosper you, not to harm you, plans to give you a future and a hope*, it said, on the page taken from Isaiah.

"I've set aside a bit of money over the years," Ardelle said. "Enough to send you to Bible school in Caronport. If you don't mind the train, you can come stay with me for holidays. The money's yours, if you decide."

After that they were quiet again, but Jonah had pocketed the words.

When he got home he hid the folded page under his mattress but carried the passage around with him in his thoughts.

"You're wrong, you know," Jonah said quietly to his father. He had been back home for nearly two months and his uncle's land had produced a better crop than his father's, giving them more money than they'd ever had. "You're wrong about people."

"You may think that now," his father said. He stood up straight and squinted until his eyes were condescending slits. He tried to work something out of his teeth with his tongue and made wet, sucking noises. "But when you get a little older and you have some brains and brats of your own, you'll see. Nothin' here in this world's worth living for. Just a few things worth dying over."

When Jonah saw Hazel for the first time, it was one of those moments. Like when, a year later, they visited the West Coast on their honeymoon and Jonah knew he should have been born near the ocean instead of an island of dirt surrounded by wheat and flax.

Jonah had finished high school at Caronport and moved across campus for college classes at Briercrest where Hazel was a year ahead of him, but a year younger. Her parents lived in Regina and had forgotten everything they ever knew about farming.

At first Jonah couldn't get Hazel to notice him. In the cafeteria, although he chose his seat so she couldn't help but see him, she usually immersed herself in a book while forking up bites of mashed potatoes, of which she always took twice as much as anyone else. He watched as other young men offered to fetch her dessert: vanilla ice cream with stewed plums. Those who were in seminary and encouraged to have a wife before entering the ministry, would sometimes sit across from her and thoughtfully open their Bibles on the table, reading as though in deep contemplation of the mysteries. Hazel wasn't the most beautiful girl on campus, but what beauty she had was knit together with a quick wit and steady peace that attracted Jonah and the others to her like mice to a sack of grain.

When Hazel would glance up from her book to see who'd sat down across from her, and when one of the young men would gather the courage to start a conversation in hopes it might lead towards sitting together at the next meal, she politely told them that she hadn't come to Briercrest to get married. Which was funny, because it was well known that Briercrest was where good Mennonite girls went to find a husband.

One day Jonah brought her an extra plate of mashed potatoes. He set it on the table and slowly pushed it towards her. Looking up from her book she laughed, a self-conscious snort that acknowledged her own ridiculousness. The two of them stayed and talked until the cafeteria matron stood at the door and jangled her key ring. Hazel told Jonah that she walked with the Lord, and Briercrest was where she had followed Him. "Yeesh — that must really make me sound like a barrel of fun!"

"Barrel of potatoes, maybe."

All through the rest of the school year Jonah was late to his first class of the morning, too busy trying to accidentally bump into Hazel on the way to hers. Sometimes she'd wave, other times she didn't see him. What began to seem plain to Jonah was that she wasn't looking. But when he noticed her in the stands one afternoon when his curling team was on the ice sheet in the old airplane hangar, he became certain that God had caused her to attend Briercrest just to meet him. Not long after, they became engaged. Jonah was twenty years old, ready to claim his uncle's house and land.

The house that once belonged to Jonah's uncle was visible from Jonah's old bedroom window in his parents' house. On top of a low hill, the structure sat higher than theirs, and Jonah had often imagined how he'd grow up to raise a different sort of family there. A family that laughed together often. There would be pictures of grandparents — his wife's parents — on the mantel above the fireplace. They'd empty loose change from their pockets into a dish by the front door to spend on ice cream, instead of locked away in a metal box kept under the wood stove, with a mouse trap set on top. In the house on the hill, the pantry would always be lined with glass jars full of plums.

When Jonah and Hazel first arrived, Jonah stood on his porch and looked down their hill, wild with grasses, towards his parents' house that was surrounded by a yard of compact dirt and strewn with orderly accumulations of broken down machinery.

Jonah's father looked over Hazel for the first time as she stood next to Jonah in their front door, twisting the thin gold ring on her finger. She was dressed in a pair of jeans and, because she hadn't been expecting company and it was a hot day in July, a blouse that was unbuttoned halfway from the bottom and tied into a knot. Her dark hair swung freely across her face.

"Doesn't seem to me she's likely to last long out here," he said to Jonah. The same way he might have talked about a cow that wasn't fat enough to produce milk.

Jonah's father had taken off his hat when he knocked on the couple's door, even though Jonah knew he had no mind to come inside. Now he hit the hat against his hand to indicate he'd said what he came to say, and a puff of dust was expelled into the air. He waved it away before he set the grubby old fedora back on his head. "Just see that she isn't a burden to me and your mother. We're too old to put up with trouble on account of someone who can't pull her own weight." At barely fifty, Jonah's father wasn't old enough to have been busy dying for so many years.

Hazel stood at the door for a moment longer before gently pushing it closed.

"We should have gone over to see them as soon as we got here," Hazel said when she turned around and faced her husband. She was anxiously unknotting her blouse and tucking it into her waistband. Jonah watched for a sign that she was hurt, or disgusted, by his father's behaviour. That she was angry at Jonah for not telling her before what kind of a miserable old bugger the man was.

"First they couldn't make it out for our wedding and now this. Your parents must feel so left out. We should go over right away and apologize." Hazel looked around her and picked up a basket of jams and crackers — a wedding gift from a favourite teacher — from the kitchen table and stepped towards the door.

"Apologize?" Jonah said. "He just insulted you. He should be the one to apologize."

"Yes. But he won't, will he?" Hazel said, surprising Jonah.

"There's no point."

"There is. Even if not for them." It didn't matter that Jonah didn't understand, because in that moment he believed her. He would have believed her if she said pigs laid eggs. And two years later, he still believed her when they had Katie. Even after his father bent over her crib and shook his head. Nobody had asked him, he said, whether he wanted to be a grandfather.

"He's sick in his heart. He can't help himself," Hazel said after Jonah's father had left.

"I suppose." Jonah lifted Katie from Hazel's arms and looked into her sleepy face. "It doesn't matter, though."

When Katie was old enough, Jonah taught her how to take fresh eggs from under their hens, the way his Aunt Ardelle had taught him. He knew, and it pleased him, that sometimes his father would be out in his own yard and see them sneaking towards the henhouse first thing in the morning, pretending they were foxes. When they came back, Hazel would meet them at the door, ready to cook the eggs. Sunny-side-up for Jonah. Scrambled for herself and Katie.

At first when Jonah woke up and couldn't hear out of his left ear, he thought he must have left it plugged with the cotton wool he used to protect it against the noise of farm machinery. Probably it had been a good joke between Hazel and Katie, and they might even have made a little bet — who would have to peel the apples for Sunday's pie — about how long it would take him to notice. He laughed at himself and wondered whether either of them thought it would be morning before he noticed his mistake.

He couldn't feel anything inside his ear, though. When he tried to peer into it using Hazel's cosmetics mirrors, he saw nothing. Just a few more wiry hairs than he'd expected, and a rim of wax around the entrance to the canal. He had thought himself more meticulous.

He covered his good ear with his hand and slammed a cabinet door. No, he wasn't deaf. Not completely. It was like listening through a pillow. Jonah slammed the door again, expecting a change, for something to shake loose and sound to rush back in. But it was the same.

In the kitchen, Jonah found Hazel busy over a pan of eggs, Katie colouring on his newspaper. The bacon grease crackled and spat, but sounded flat.

"Sunny side?" Hazel said.

Jonah realized he was staring at her, and that she'd noticed. He was often given to long, appreciative looks — sometimes he still couldn't believe she was his — but this was different. Seeing her dressed in last night's rumpled pyjamas, her hair twisted into a careless knot, his mouth dried up and his breath became shallow. What would she do if something were to happen to him now? How would she survive out here, living next to his parents? Or would she leave with Katie and never think of him again?

Jonah put his hand over his good ear as Hazel repeated her question, but all he heard was her muffled voice, with no words.

"Fine," he said. He sat down at the table across from Katie and watched her darling face, the map of freckles sprayed across her nose.

Katie looked up at her father, and when he gazed into her eyes, she giggled. "Daddy, don't look at me like that," she said.

"Like what?"

"Like you love me."

Jonah felt as though his chest had been caught in a fan belt. "I'm not supposed to love you?" he said, his voice becoming sharp.

Katie knit her eyebrows together. "You're funny today," she said and looked back to the picture she was drawing.

"My newspapers aren't for your colouring," Jonah said. He snatched the paper from underneath her crayons, sending them flying. The one she'd been using left a mark on the table.

"What's gotten into you this morning?" Hazel said. She set a plate with two eggs, a heap of bacon, and toast in front of him.

"Nothing. I'd just like to read the paper before it becomes a colouring book."

Jonah lowered his head to look at his eggs and thought about how he and Hazel were spoiling Katie. He made up his mind right then to be more firm.

As April became May and the last days of cold gave way to spring weather, Jonah convinced himself he was fine. No need to worry.

He helped Hazel sweep out the front porch. It was Katie's favourite place, where she had finally decided to crawl for the first time. She'd been determined to visit the row of Hazel's colourful rubber boots lined up against the outside wall.

In May, Hazel always moved her sewing into the porch. Katie was kept busy sorting buttons and helping unspool colourful bolts of fabric to become slipcovers and pillowcases and pleated bed skirts. At six years old Katie wasn't much of a help yet, but Hazel sometimes let her press the sewing machine pedal from under the table while Hazel guided the fabric under the racing needle.

This year the two of them were making new curtains, all in some shade of blue, for every room in the house. Hazel preferred pale, solid colours that let light in, rather than the heavy drapes Jonah's mother favoured, or the traditional farmsy patterns often used by the local wives. Something Jonah discovered last year when he brought home a length of blue gingham from a yard sale. Hazel laughed, a sound that was light and watery, and said she'd use it to make tablecloths.

"I love you for trying," she'd said.

"Then just wait a minute to see what else I have." Jonah went back out to his truck and carried in a new sewing machine — the woman who sold him the gingham had decided she preferred her old manual Singer, a heavy black model that had to be pumped into action. She gave him a good price on the new one, but he would gladly have gone back and paid her twice when he saw the look on Hazel's face.

"What am I going to do with the old one?" she said, already making room on her sewing table for the new machine.

"I'll use it," Jonah announced, pleased with himself.

"You?" Hazel crossed her arms loosely and laughed, a sound that made Jonah think of sun showers. "You've never made a stitch your whole life, let alone a straight row of them."

"I can learn to mend my own overalls, and you can save the good machine for your fancy material. Really, if I can drive a combine, I think I can do this."

The next day though, when he tried to make sense of the machine, he misthreaded the bobbin and forgot to lock down the presser foot. He stepped on the pedal as though he was starting a truck engine. When Hazel and Katie ran out into the porch to see why he had yelped, Jonah tried to keep them from seeing the mass of black thread that looked like a patch of crabgrass sewn into the seat of his pants. They all laughed until their sides hurt. Afterwards, they drove into Swift Current for ice cream. Katie's favourite was pistachio. She liked that it was green.

It had been weeks since Jonah first noticed the quietness in his ear. For the most part, he learned to compensate. So when the phone rang in their kitchen, he put it to his good ear and heard his mother's voice.

"Come over, will you," she said. It wasn't a question, and she hung up as soon as she said it.

"What's wrong with your hearing?" Jonah's mother took one look at him on the back doorstep and asked this, before he could even say hello.

"What do you mean?" Jonah said, feeling suddenly exposed.

"I've seen enough old people come towards me with just one ear or the other to know when they've gone deaf."

"It's nothing. Just some water from the shower."

"If you say so." She didn't seem convinced but was unwilling to pursue the matter. "I heard Hazel's up there making herself some new curtains, eh?"

"Blue," he said, unable to think of something more interesting. He looked around, taking in the perpetual sameness of his parents' house. Even though his mother had recently changed her own curtains, they weren't much different from the heavy yellow panels he'd known his whole life.

The new curtains were from the house of an old farmer who had lately died. Jonah's mother considered them her due for being enlisted, along with a few other church ladies, to help with the cleaning.

"Well, here, then. I owe her for the Saskatoons she picked for me last summer. I have no use for fruit, but I won't have her thinking I forgot the favour." She went into the pantry and with the inside of her foot shoved a box across the kitchen floor. The cardboard was waxy and its bottom peppered in grit. The sound it made on the floor scraped into Jonah's good ear, which he couldn't help but turn towards the noise. "They're not blue, but I don't see any good reason these won't keep out the sun just as well. She can save her material and make something useful for her and the girl to wear to church. Noticed you weren't there last Sunday."

As he walked back up the hill to his own house, weighed down with his mother's box, Jonah thought about Hazel and quickened his pace. Halfway home, he wondered why his mother had noticed his hearing and Hazel had not.

"What did Mom want?" Hazel said when Jonah let the porch's storm door spring shut behind him. He dropped the box with the curtains into a corner and heard a one-dimensional thud.

"She thought you could use these," he said, looking from the bile-coloured drapes in the box, to the length of watery blue fabric draped across Hazel's lap. She was getting ready to sew. "Something about paying you back for some Saskatoons?"

"That's nice." Hazel glanced at the box and scrunched her nose. She seemed amused, the same way as when one of the old people from nearby pressed a greasy paper bag full of fried New Year's cookies into her hands, a thank-you for a visit. She'd thank them as though the simple-minded gratitude of farm-folk was endearing. But who was she to think that? And now, Jonah thought, she was making the same face over his mother's gift. His mother, who wasn't grateful for the berries, just worried that anyone might think she owed them.

"Uh huh," Jonah said. He paused, turning his next words over on his tongue. They didn't taste right. He didn't even mean them. After all, he intended to throw the box of curtains into the back of his truck and get rid of them the next time he went to the nuisance yard. He didn't care about them. "What are you going to do with these?" he said.

"Salvation Army, I guess."

"Really?"

"Sure, why?"

"She's going to want to know what you did with them."

"I don't like them," Hazel said simply. She was threading a needle and had a length of blue thread between her teeth, but stopped to give him her attention. Katie, who Jonah could just see under the sewing table, had stitched together two squares of fabric, with holes left open for the head and arms of her favourite doll to fit through. She was about to come out, would have stood up and leaned against his leg in the way she always did, but instead shrunk back farther under the table. She had dropped her needle. Jonah could see it, a thin silver splinter sticking out of the rug.

"Katie," he said, crouching down to look her in the face. "Do you see that?" He pointed to the needle, a trail of red thread looped through its eye.

"I dropped it. Mommy's teaching me."

"Teaching you to drop needles where people can step on them?"

"No." He could see she was confused. Unused to being scolded. Not with the way they always treated her, as though she was a treasure on loan to them from God. As Jonah looked at his daughter, he saw how little it would take to turn her confusion into crying. He tried to stop himself. After all, he was wearing boots, so the needle couldn't have harmed him.

"What if Daddy stepped on that, got it stuck in his foot, right into the bone, and had to pull it out with the pliers?" he said, and watched as Katie's eyes began to blur under a film of tears.

"Jonah!" Hazel hissed under her breath. "What are you doing?"

She squeezed his shoulder, hard, and he glanced up from where he crouched and saw Hazel looking at him as though he was the crazy man down the hill. Like he hadn't just said something perfectly reasonable. Still, he considered apologizing to Katie, lifting her from under the table and saying he was sorry, that she just needed to be more careful. After that, once Katie's quivering bottom lip was stilled, he'd take his mother's curtains away, but not before he'd lean over Hazel, sweep her hair aside and kiss behind her ear. He'd whisper an apology to her, too, and she'd forgive him. Of course she'd forgive him.

As Jonah stood up, he knocked Hazel's scissors off the table. The blades opened into straight-edged jaws, but he barely heard them hit the floor. He cringed at the lack of sound and instinctively put his hand up to his ear. For a moment, he allowed himself to believe, again, that there might be something very wrong with him. And neither Hazel nor Katie, so busy with their own small concerns, cared enough to notice.

"I expect to see my mother's drapes up by tonight," he said. He kicked the box and left for the barn. Hazel got up to go after him, but she was wearing slippers and stopped at the end of the walk. Jonah ignored her when she called after him.

When Jonah came home later that evening, it was almost dark, and he saw from the outside of the house that his mother's old curtains were hung. Light from the kitchen spilled, jaundiced, between the seams, and the curtains themselves looked harsh and stiff, the fabric bristly with sun stains on the lining. He remembered that they always smelled harshly yellow in his parents' house, like strong pollen.

Now, when Jonah opened the door to his own house and stepped inside, he stood stiff as a switch. After a while, he managed to sit down, but for the rest of the evening didn't say anything. He just stared at the drapes in silence, picking dead skin from his lips.

By the next morning, Hazel had removed the old curtains and Jonah didn't ask what she did with them. In their place were the new blue panels she'd finished sewing the day before.

"I'm sorry," Jonah whispered into Hazel's hair. He had found her still in her pyjamas, her body soft with sleep, standing over a pot of oatmeal. She looked the way she used to when they were first married and he would wrap himself around her from behind while she stirred. "I'll make it up to the two of you. I promise." To Katie, waiting quietly at the table, he said, "How'd you and Mommy like to go for a drive today?"

With Katie in the backseat, Jonah reached beside him and squeezed Hazel's hand. As much a reassurance for himself as her. She turned towards him and he saw a new uncertainty tugging at her eyes and mouth. She was entitled to it, he thought, after the way he'd behaved over those damn curtains.

Jonah looked at Katie in the rear view mirror. "Guessed where we're going yet?"

"Swift Current?" she said, unsure.

"Nope. Some place you've never been. Even Mom doesn't know." Jonah grinned and turned his attention back to the road. Though he still couldn't hear out of the one ear, he felt a lightness returning to him. He had overcome his worry, and nothing could bring him down.

But Jonah hadn't considered that the tourist amenities at Cypress Hills wouldn't be open yet in the second week of May. The hut where visitors could rent paddleboats and canoes in the summer was boarded up. As were the hamburger and ice cream stands. It was cold, too, when they arrived, with sharp gusts of wind blowing off the lake.

"Damn it." Jonah jolted the car into park and dropped his hands back onto the steering wheel as they rocked to a stop.

"What are we doing here?" Hazel said, reminding him that Katie was in the back seat.

"Well." He looked around. "I guess we don't need cheeseburgers and a paddleboat to have a good time. We'll go for a walk around the lake and look at all the cabins." He got out of the car and opened Katie's door. "Isn't this nice, sweetheart?" He took her hand and started to walk towards the lake.

"I'm cold. I want to go home," Katie said. She was already shivering.

"Where's your coat?"

"I didn't bring it," she said, looking up at him as though he'd know where to find a new one. Jonah pictured where her coat was at home, on a hook in the mudroom. It would have been so simple for her to take it. Why hadn't she? He and Hazel had taught her better than to be so forgetful. For a moment he felt as though having identified the problem would make it go away. Katie would have her coat. And for God's sake, maybe if a few businesses opened a little earlier, more people would come.

"Why didn't you put it on?" Jonah said. He let go of her hand and clenched both of his into fists, the colour of his knuckles draining to white.

Hazel came between Katie and Jonah. "Maybe we should just turn around and go home. We had a nice drive together. I think it's enough."

Jonah knew she was being reasonable. Yet something flared. Like an explosion seen in slow motion, he could feel it expand but was helpless to stop it.

"We're not going to let her mistake ruin this for everyone," he said. He put up a finger to silence Hazel and walked back to the car, unlocked the trunk and began to rummage around until he found a pair of his old garage pants, blotched with machine oil.

When he wrapped them around Katie's shoulders she slumped under the stiff weight.

"I'm not really that cold," she said, but it came out chopped up. "I-m n-ot re-all-y th-a-t c-old."

Hazel took off her own jacket, bundled it around Katie and picked her up. "It's not her mistake. If you'd told me where we were going, I would have known what to bring. For that matter, you knew — why didn't you grab her coat?"

"She's old enough to think for herself once in a while. And if she can't, it's your job to make sure she has what she needs."

Hazel put Katie down but continued to hold on to her as she spoke. "Something's wrong. Something's been wrong for a while now. I've been waiting for you to tell me, but you need to do it now. What is it?"

"It's nothing. Nothing's wrong. Does something have to be wrong to expect a little gratitude?" Jonah got into the car and drove away without looking back at Hazel and Katie, whom he'd left at the edge of the lake. When he returned for them an hour later, they were huddled together on a large rock, throwing stones into the water. Nobody said anything until they were home.

"How about I make us some *varenyky* for supper? I think there's still some in the freezer," Hazel said to Katie as they climbed the few wooden steps into the porch and took off their shoes.

Katie nodded and looked back at Jonah, her cheeks brightening a little. Jonah smiled thinly, deliberately, before he went past them and into the bathroom where he closed the door. In the mirror he saw that the contented creases at the corners of his eyes had begun to fade, replaced by the beginnings of channels that appeared across his forehead and between his brows. He covered his ear with his hand and looked away.

Later that night, Jonah woke up and found Hazel on her knees, praying in front of the picture window in their bedroom. He knew without listening to his wife's whispers that she was busy thanking God for something. Worse though, he knew she was praying for him. He turned away, waiting to be pulled back down into sleep.

A few weeks after the drive to Cypress, Katie peeked in on Jonah as he sat in a chair in front of his bedroom window, staring at the last narrow band of sunset.

"Daddy?"

"When's the last time you had an ear infection?" he asked. She took a step towards him, but when he didn't turn to look at her, or hold out his hand for her to come, she stayed near the door.

"I don't know. A long time?" Katie said, though Jonah knew she'd had more than her share of them.

Jonah let his head fall forward, as though a string at the back of his neck had been cut. He waved towards the door for Katie to leave. She didn't though, and Jonah saw her crouch into the shadow of the bed. He'd already decided that the only thing that could be wrong with his ear was a tumour. He had convinced himself of it, feeding the idea until it grew and invaded every other thought. He had cancer. The tumour was growing and pressing against his eardrum. Soon, if it hadn't already, it would spread to his brain and bones and that would be it.

"Cancer," he said to himself, loud enough for Katie to hear. "Do you know what surgery is? They'll put me on a table and cut into my head. Remove as much as they can, but it won't be enough." Jonah nearly laughed when he thought how the disease that had taken his Uncle Elias had skipped over his father — probably his insides were too vinegary for the disease to survive in — and settled for him.

"It's probably nothing serious," Hazel said the next morning when Jonah told her what he suspected. "You haven't even seen the doctor."

Jonah sat on a paper-covered examination table in the doctor's office, holding his breath as the doctor peered into his ear. He closed his eyes and thought about how his uncle was prepared to accept God's will. But Jonah wasn't. He was furious with God, and had told Him so.

"Why don't you take that pickled old shit down the hill?" Jonah had shouted up to the sky before driving to town. Then he hung his head and wept. "I've become a better man than him. I'm a good husband. A good father. I don't deserve this."

Jonah was quiet when he talked to the doctor, describing what had happened with as few words as possible.

"Aha, well, there we have it," the doctor said after he'd shone a light into Jonah's ear. He selected a pair of slender metal tweezers from a drawer and slid them inside Jonah's ear canal. "This little bugger must've been looking for a safe place. Wait, wait. Hold still, then, or you'll have part of him left in there, and my tweezers lodged in your eardrum." He probed gently and Jonah felt something inside shift and be withdrawn. He didn't have a chance to ask what it was before sound rushed back into his ear like a cool breath. He waited quietly for the doctor to flush warm water into his ear and drain it into a crescent-shaped bowl.

"All done," the doctor said, peering into the basin, sloshing the liquid back and forth until he seemed satisfied. "All anatomy present and accounted for."

Jonah looked inside the bowl the doctor held out. Among other parts, an anther and a slender black insect leg floated together with globs of wax. On the table, a large luna moth had been set aside with the tweezers, its stained-glass wings crumpled against its body.

Jonah stared at the moth for a long while, as though it would reveal something. Finally, he slid off the examination table, nodded towards the insect and said, "I want to keep it. Can you put it in a jar?"

At home, Jonah put the moth in a drawer of his night table. He sat on the edge of the bed, rested his face in his hands. Even though it turned out to be nothing, he still felt as though he'd narrowly missed sharing his uncle's fate. And nearly lost something else, as well.

Jonah didn't tell Hazel about the moth that night. He woke early the next morning, before Hazel or Katie, and thought he could hear the moth fluttering in his ear. The sound was like whispers. The words, if there were any, were empty.

As the room began to take shape in the grey light before dawn, Jonah opened the drawer beside his bed and took out the moth, still in the specimen jar from the doctor.

Jonah slid his feet to the floor, quietly left the room and walked through the house until he was outside, standing on his front porch. From where he stood, he could see his father down the hill, walking away from their old barn, his back bent, a heavy pail of milk in each hand. Jonah looked at the moth again. Suddenly he couldn't remember why he had wanted to keep it.

ASHES

LIBBY WOULD RATHER BE IN THE garden. It's almost warm enough this April. As teasings of green push up through the soil to suggest early spring, she feels a winter's worth of longing to plant the garden, walk with bare feet through warm mud, take root alongside the seeds she harvested from last year's best squash and melons. She intends to grow tomatoes this year as well, although she has sometimes been accused of giving them too much space that could otherwise be seeded with more sensible vegetables. The kind that grow in straight rows with modest coverings of husks and pods and rinds. Or potatoes, ugly but underground.

Tomatoes make Anke nervous. The way they become vulnerable to frost at the first hint of ripening. Their shameless red and soft flesh that yields to the slightest pressure, their gel-enveloped seeds. There was a time when she picked and ate them in the afternoon, warm from the vine. Now she presses them into sterilized jars, tempers their sweetness with a boiling salt-and-vinegar brine.

Besides tomato red there are other colours Anke finds disturbing. Blue, like the scattered shards of cobalt pottery scattered through the far garden. And yellow. Tuscany yellow. The name of a paint she'd once chosen for one of the bedrooms.

Unlike Libby, Anke is a sure voice for practicality. But, since Matthew went and married Libby anyway, Anke won't say a word to him about it now. Tell him that girls like Libby inevitably come to grief. That their careless, barefoot-in-the-spring ways, their enthusiasm, undoes them. And Anke's not willing to explain how she knows this.

"It's been so warm. Almost like home on the coast," Libby says to Anke, even though she knows that referring so often to her life before Saskatchewan irritates her mother-in-law. "I saw Meryl next door putting out trellises for her sweet peas."

"Meryl?" Anke says, as though she has never heard the name.

"Mrs. Larsen's daughter-in-law. Remember? There were such lovely peonies at Jake and Meryl's wedding last summer. All different pinks. I'm thinking of trying to hybridize a new variety to name after her." Libby knows Anke wishes she would attach herself to the daughters of Anke's friends rather than their son's wives.

"What I know is that you sure-as-sin don't want anyone to think of you in the same breath as that senseless girl," Anke says. "I went to pay her a visit after she moved in over there, you know, and found her popping pansies into her mouth like she was eating lettuce. And acting as though there was nothing at all strange about it. Why would you want to name a flower . . . " Her voice trails off as she sees Libby heaping fruit into a pie shell.

"Libby. You'll be using up the last of my good peaches on just one pie if you keep that up. I want at least six to put in the freezer. And besides, it just doesn't seem right to pile fruit all up on top of itself like that, does it?"

Anke bites her tongue to keep from wasting a short sermon on "immoral fruit." Libby doesn't appreciate good sense.

Deflated, Libby spoons most of the fruit from the pie shell back into the bowl and spreads the thin layer of remaining peaches over the bottom before fitting on the top crust. She crimps the edges and wonders when Anke learned to be so tight. Even sleep seems a necessity Anke resents when there is work that could be done. Libby though, as she sits by the kitchen window and works on the peaches, is in a good mood, wanting peace on such a lovely day when everything outside seems filled with possibilities. She smoothes a hand over the small new curve under her apron and looks outside.

"There's no need for showing that off," Anke says, noticing Libby's fingers moving under the pleated, curtain-like fabric tied at her waist. She lately presented Libby with a set of seven such aprons, one for each day and a special one for Sunday. In case they should be surprised in the kitchen by neighbours, she explained, or the nosey farm boy hired to help in the fields this year. "I myself stayed out of sight when young and expecting," she says. "Although I suppose things were different then — probably even in cities — "

Anke doesn't approve of city girls moving to farms. Not even Libby, who has a college degree in plants but no sense of how fickle they can be, especially on the prairies. Libby, who Anke believes vexed Matthew's father into his grave last summer with all her organic and hybrid ideas. He might have lived another year, she suspects, if not pressed to change his ways. But Anke never brings that up. Or how, as a widow, she had no choice but to sell her house to her son and let Libby behave as though it was her own to do with as she pleases — while Anke lives like an unwelcome guest in the upstairs bedroom, pretending tiredness at seven-thirty in the evening so she isn't in their way. Do they appreciate her sacrifice? It doesn't matter, she tells herself; generosity should be performed without thought of rewards in heaven.

And soon, God willing, there will be an infant and what a chore that will be, to undo all the permissive upbringing and unchecked affection she's sure the child will receive. So, although she has lately begun to feel pain in her chest when it is cold and in her head when it is hot, she is determined to live long enough to see that her grandchild isn't raised without some good German sense.

"I've been thinking about a name for the child," Anke says. "Abraham. After his grandfather. It only seems right."

"I don't think we want to name a baby after someone who's dead," Libby says too quickly. "And besides, we think it's a girl."

"There's never been a girl born first in my family."

It's not entirely true. Not true at all, in fact. There was her Ruth, but too few people remember her. And now Libby's quick refusal to consider Abraham has injured Anke, and she imagines how her son must have been manipulated into agreeing to forget his father. The same way he was seduced into marrying this girl who, with all her untried ideas about farming, is practically a foreigner. She knows she should have insisted harder that he go to school in Saskatchewan. Only nonsense comes from wanting to live by the ocean. And Libby is all nonsense, unlike the girls he would have met closer to home. Steady girls, with parents who know where they've come from.

Libby considers herself "Canadian," as if saying so means anything. A Swedish-Dutch mother and a mostly Swiss father. Who can even keep track of such genetic clutter?

"How about Abel?" Libby says.

"So, you won't use the name of my dead husband. But you'll curse a child with the name of the first person murdered on this earth."

"I just thought — "

"What? That it's almost like Abraham? I'm sure in your mind it is."

Libby considers suggesting Jezebel for a girl, but decides it won't make either of them feel better.

"And don't go thinking up any of those new-age names you west-coast girls are so infatuated with. I won't have a grandchild named Sunshine or Sand Dollar or God knows what else. A solid European name is best in Saskatchewan. German, since that's what he'll be."

Anke wants to say the name Ruth, but it sticks in her throat like a thistle, and she swallows hard to force it back down.

The kitchen is too hot, the oven breathing out heat for the baking of Anke's half-inch-thick pies. Although Libby knows what thoughts it will prompt in her mother-in-law's mind, she slips outside through the kitchen's back door, where she inhales slow draughts of spring air, testing it for substance like a vintner pondering young wine for a sense of its emerging notes of oak and florals. This will be her third summer here, so far away from the mountains and mild coastal weather. Where farming takes place in occasional valleys, not all over the province, on expansive fields flat as an unspooled carpet. Like here, where her wedding to Matthew, like everything else, had waited until after the harvest.

And then came the shock of her first real winter, when the temperature on the thermometer meant nothing if there was wind. And there was always wind.

It happened on a January walk, when she went out into what began as a soft, insulating snowfall but changed suddenly into a blizzard that whipped snow sideways and froze the moisture in her lungs, that Libby found an abandoned outbuilding at the far corner of the farm.

With a small wood-burning stove and stack of dry wood and matches, Libby was able to make a fire and keep warm until the storm passed. And later, in the spring, she claimed and restored the place into a haven for herself and her plants. She imagines children playing there — two girls and a boy — planting seeds for red and yellow carrots and candy cane beets. Chasing one another on the freshly cut grass, stopping to sing "Ring Around the Rosie". Tumbling down, laughing, after ashes, ashes.

We all fall down, Libby sings, thinking of Anke and wondering why she'd had only one child. A daughter might have softened her.

Anke only said so once, but she disapproved of Libby's plans for the shed. Strangely possessive of a place she never visited, Libby thought. But because Anke kept her disdain to a few scornful looks, Libby went out to swish up cobwebs and push dust out the door in what felt like her first true act of housekeeping. Now the walls are hung with new shelves of old wood displaying her collection of glass cloches — from tiny domes that warm delicate young sprouts to giant mute bells that help capture sunlight to grow her tomatoes. Libby thinks of the cloches as keepers of garden memory; she believes in their ability to remember plants. The same way a woman's body remembers its children.

Libby has walked farther than she meant to, her feet finding the path to the shed. It always seems to happen like this when she lets her mind wander. The shed comes into view unexpectedly, rewarding her with the sight of its weathered frame and gentle windward lean.

I wonder what these walls remember? Libby thinks as she steps up into their shade. She touches the lintel as if to remind the shed who she is.

When she first found it that winter it contained nothing but a packet of unviable poppy seeds and a few clay pots, now filled with fragments of blue pottery she found everywhere in the adjoining square of garden. The shards told her that this place hadn't always been a secret, though it was impossible to know when it had last been used. What was certain, was if the shards were left in the garden, their sharp edges would threaten the roots of tomatoes and pansies and, even if the plants survived, they'd be unable to bloom.

From inside the shed, the old sunken glass windows, etched and altered by decades of dust storms, will never be clear. When Libby looks through them, the world appears as if under water.

For all its suggestions of former use, Libby senses the garden shed has begun to accept her, a transplant, struggling to thrive among sturdier stalks. Still, it seems determined to keep its secrets.

In the kitchen, Anke — though she prefers being left alone to do things the right way the first time — is working herself into satisfied indignation over Libby's absence. *Where is that girl, anyway? She should want to be here and help. To learn how women in this family do things. And that includes learning how to take care of my son the way he's been used to.*

Such a dear boy, she says to herself. For all his soft-heartedness and lack of sense. She can't blame him for that. It was Libby who took advantage and didn't know her place, who made him think he should come in from the fields and still have to do more. Like clearing the table or wiping his crumbs off the counter or rinsing the bar of soap when he's dirtied it. Such little things. It would be easier for Libby to do them herself rather than always nag. So when Anke notices the soap is covered in muddy bubbles that puddle on the sink's crackled porcelain, she gives it all a rinse. *There, you see?* She has flushed an argument down the drain by doing the chore herself.

Anke knows her pies are done by the particular aroma of hot fruit. Years of baking have given her a sense about such things, a knack that once allowed her to keep a sparse, uncluttered kitchen. Now there are drawers full of new gadgets. A bouquet of whisks when one fork would do. Timers and thermometers for everything, when Anke can throw together a six-course meal and bring it to the table just as everyone suddenly realizes they're hungry. All without looking at a clock.

And that's another thing. Libby has a clock for every room and always wears a watch, constantly checking to make sure they're all set at the exact same time. As if the world revolves around those clocks and not the other way around. Anke has woken up every day for fifty years at 5:15 AM, and she doesn't need anyone to wake or tell her the time.

Lost in her thoughts of Libby, Anke has almost whipped the cream into butter. Her favourite fork for the task lashes deftly through the thickening foam, the sound of it changing, becoming dull as the cream's volume increases in her mother's old enamelled bowl, chipped by two generations of everyday use. She won't add sugar or vanilla to her cream. No need for such extravagance. Especially on a Tuesday.

Outside Libby watches a robin settle on a fence post and shuffle its wings into place, its red breast pushed out to announce its springtime intentions. Libby once discovered a dead chick fallen from its twig-and-fluff nest which was littered with broken blue egg shells. The chick's featherless wings were splayed as if ready for flight, while above, its siblings in the nest squawked for worms to be thrust into their open mouths.

"The world is cruel like that," Libby says to the robin. It cocks its head and looks at her closely with one dark eye, then the other. Anke would say the same. About the world being cruel. Except she wouldn't stop along her way to feel sorrow. Nothing is safe until it's dead, is how she'd put it. Libby buried the chick beneath the tree and placed a stone on its grave.

Inside of her, Libby's baby is still, when only yesterday she felt it flutter its limbs. The doctor assured her last week that a bit of blood wasn't much to worry about. So long as there wasn't more. And there hasn't been.

"Don't go getting attached before it's time," Anke had told her, but Libby was fully committed to this child from the moment she held the pregnancy test and watched the indicator strip turn blue. That was more than sixteen weeks ago.

Libby turns towards the sun. "Do you feel that?" she says. She touches her belly, but there's no response. Like when the lights go out in a storm, she struggles to sense the outline of something that recently seemed so clear. It won't come to her and, instead, she tries to remember what it was that had driven her out of the kitchen.

"No point trying to help now," Anke says without looking up from a sink full of dishes. "Just change out of that dusty dress before supper. And if you can manage that, then set the table. You may as well know I've invited Mrs. Larsen and her son from next door. Seems his new wife ran off to visit her mother."

"Is Meryl's mother all right?" Libby says, but Anke continues as if Libby hasn't spoken.

"I don't know what that girl was thinking, going off with nothing at all made to eat. Old Mrs. Larsen isn't the woman, or the cook, she used to be."

Old Mrs. Larsen's only problem is that she's sour, Libby is tempted to say, imagining the woman's miserly, puckered face. Small wonder Anke is her most faithful friend. Libby pushes the thought away, concentrating on a wave of fatigue.

"I'll set the table, Anke. I'm going to eat later, though. I'm not feeling very well all of a sudden," Libby says, and it's the truth. The thought of sitting down to supper with a pair of condescending old ladies makes her head feel light. Already, the room seems to be moving sideways.

The doctor said not to worry, she tells herself again. But was that really what he'd said? Right now she only remembers hearing her child's heart beating for the first time. The cold tape across her belly, measuring a new pound of progress.

"And what excuse should I make for you?" Anke says, provoked by the scent of outdoors on Libby's clothes. "No, you'll sit and eat with us. You can have your nap once our company's gone."

Libby leans against the table and feels vacant, has to stop to count on her fingers how many plates and how many forks she needs to complete her task.

"Call me when they come," Libby says without looking back. Moments later, she examines her face in the bathroom mirror. It seems featureless. As though her eyes and mouth and nose need to be pencilled in. She gives in to a compelling need to sit down.

She tells herself she's just lightheaded from her walk, and lets the coolness of the tiled floor catch her slowly. Such a beautiful blue. She's always thought the mosaic, with its patterns of cerulean and cobalt, its reliefs of yellow, a strange choice for Anke, when everything else in the house is so plain. Her husband once told her the floor was his mother's own design, although this is the first time she's thought the tiles familiar in another way. But it refuses to become clear to her as she tries to make sense of a resonating ache, an inward physical agony that feels like both pain and grief.

She follows the pain with both hands, from the rise of her belly down between the cradle of her hips to her pelvis and beneath the sturdy elastic of her new maternity underwear, where her fingers find blood, warm and sticky and thick.

"Anke!" she calls, too softly at first, her voice growing louder and higher-pitched with each wave of pain that pauses only to surge through her back until she feels she will crack open like a gourd splitting in the sun. She leans and slides into the discharge.

"What's this?" Anke says at the door. "What are you doing down there?" She steps closer, trying to see what Libby is staring at. Why she's curled on the cold floor, her fingers exploring the tiles.

Libby lifts her head, then lays it back down, unable to hold its weight. She presses her wrists to her forehead, smearing it with blood, and begins to cry.

"Oh," Anke says, seeing more blood on the floor, a shallow pool spreading out from underneath Libby. She should have known. In fact, she tells herself that she had known and had chosen to ignore her intuition. The way she knew when they sent her daughter home twenty years ago, saying the fever which was present before her fall and the blood from her nose that stopped only to start again were not unusual symptoms for a two-year-old. A bug and a bump; that's how the doctor had referred to it. And assured Anke that such typical childhood incidents were like vaccinations. They would, in the end, make the girl stronger.

"Well, I suppose it wasn't meant to be. And you're not the first to — " Anke doesn't finish the sentence. She reaches under the sink for a stack of old towels. She presses a cold wet cloth into Libby's hands and bends to examine her, finding a tiny lifeless form in the puddle between Libby's trembling legs.

With a pair of scissors taken from Libby's bathroom drawer, Anke severs the link between mother and fetus. A girl, just as Libby predicted. Tiny. Barely a person. With translucent skin and eyelids that will never open. Arms and legs too fragile to handle with her own suddenly clumsy hands. She gently places the baby in her palm and squints to count its fingers and toes.

"She would have been perfect, Libby," Anke says. But before she can show her, Libby has another contraction and is thrust into another spasm of pain.

"It's almost over," Anke says, tenderly placing her granddaughter on a soft towel and covering her with a washcloth. She takes Libby's hand.

After Libby's womb has emptied, Anke helps her into bed. "I'll call the doctor and ask if there's anything else we should do," Anke says, her voice falling as she remembers that they're still expecting company and it will be up to her to make the necessary excuses. "And I'll tell the Larsens you've had a bit of a headache from being outside," she adds. "No sense them knowing everything that goes on around here."

She sets a tumbler of water and an aspirin on the nightstand next to Libby and arranges more towels underneath her before going back to the kitchen.

When Matthew comes in from the field, Anke is carrying a mop and a bucket full of chemical-smelling water towards the bathroom. She had hoped to clean up before he came, so he wouldn't overreact. But he has surprised her by being early, and now there is nothing to do but tell him what happened. "I'm sorry, I would have come to find you," she says when his questions become accusing, "but I'd have had to leave Libby alone. The doctor has been here and will see Libby again in the morning."

Anke lets him go and remains in the bathroom doorway long after he's gone to be with Libby. Another father too late for the death of his daughter.

Anke mops her blue and yellow tiles, smeared once again with blood. She knows the ceramic won't stain. Even the broken ones, scattered behind the shed, remain true to their colour.

"Libby at least had me," Anke says to herself. She touches her face, surprised to find it wet with tears. When Anke lost her child, she was alone and afraid, watching Ruth's blood pool on the mosaic floor. It streamed into the runnels of grout, where it clotted and dried. Later, she had begged her husband to tear up the floor, but he insisted on simply scrubbing it clean with bleach. That's when all her intentions for improving the house were put away. After Ruth's death, she would allow only what was necessary. Sturdy, practical fittings and drab colours. None of the sunny Tuscan yellows or saturated blues she loved. No red. Only beige, the colour of old wax.

But the tiles remained, reminding her of how much could be lost if she cared too much. In truth, she was glad to move upstairs last summer where there were fewer memories. Little to remind her of anything. Especially not of the daughter who made her think in colours.

"The world is cruel like that," Anke says, stiffening herself so she can welcome her guests. Suddenly, her thin peach pie seems stingy, not sensible. And Old Mrs. Larsen looks just old.

Anke hesitates, removes a plate from the table. She's glad that Libby has always had more sense than to listen to her pessimism.

Libby has not slept. Not even with the prescription Matthew picked up. The pills make her feel vague, not sleepy. She's lain awake two nights in a row watching her husband, wondering how he can bury a child and then just close his eyes. Without anyone to tell her the answer, she listens to the noises the house makes. Until now she has never noticed. Its old bones settle like sighs. Like Anke, who so often sighs before withdrawing into silence.

Libby hears Anke's feet touch the floor upstairs and knows it's 5:15 AM without looking at the clock. She expects to hear her mother-in-law next in the kitchen, lighting the stove for her percolator and dropping a slice of bread in the toaster. Instead, Libby hears the shush of her bedroom door being pushed over the carpet.

A long moment passes before Anke says, "Libby? I need to show you something." Anke knows without asking that her daughter-in-law is awake. Otherwise, she wouldn't have come.

Libby wraps herself in the mud-brown velour robe Matthew gave her last year for Christmas. The one Anke had picked out from the Sears catalogue and ordered, as always, without first asking her son.

Outside, the air is still and fresh with moisture. Pale yellow light has steeped the horizon in the exact shade of camomile tea.

The women walk side-by-side, Anke carefully guiding Libby, and Libby allowing herself to be led like a child.

"I thought it would disappear with enough time," Anke says quietly when they finally stop in front of the potting shed. In the early light, it looks restored. Not new, but as though well-rested after a night of good dreams.

"I used to love walking down to this shed. It was the one place that felt like my own. I thought my daughter and I would share it — "

Libby stops and whispers, "Daughter?"

Anke nods and looks away. "Ruth wasn't even two when we lost her. Afterwards, I tried to forget. I thought I was supposed to. But forgetting someone completely takes even more stubbornness than I have."

Anke looks at the shed and all the life brought back to it. Like a grave someone's tended after long neglect.

"There's blue pottery in the garden," Libby says after a while. "I've collected most of it."

"We had too many tiles. Enough to do two bathroom floors," Anke says. "After Ruth died, I smashed the rest and scattered them here. I cleaned out the shed and refused to let anyone go near it." She takes a deep breath. "I'm glad someone's growing flowers in there again."

"I think Ruth is a lovely name," Libby says. She opens the door to the shed. Reaches for Anke's hand. As they step inside, she points to a row of young plants, still in their pots, their green berries shedding the last of their umbilical blooms. "My tomatoes are growing."

Anke can almost taste them.

Ice House

ALTHOUGH THE ICE HOUSE AT THE back of the butcher shop has been empty for more than a year, the smell of the meat it once kept frozen is still encased in the wooden maze of meat lockers. Ani steps through the open door, which is heavy and thick like the door of a vault, into the once-familiar alleys of dead ends. She shines a small circle of light ahead of her and instead of a young woman home from college, engaged to be married, she's twelve years old again.

Tracing her way by memory she makes two right turns and a left past a second bank of lockers before taking another right into the old ice-storage room. For years the room was stacked with crumbling pyramids of bagged ice, made by two machines kept near the front of the store. It was Ani's job, after school, to scoop it into plastic bags. Afterwards, she would push them down a long cement hallway to the ice house in a rusted grocer's cart that dripped melt-water from one frozen room to the next. The wheels, which squealed but were never greased, had gradually deepened decades-old furrows in the plank floor, its grain swollen and split at the rings by water that had seeped in and frozen. After so many years of damp, the wood became soft and splintery, as though covered in hangnails.

"Ani?" her mother calls, her voice distant. She's in the hallway, just outside the ice house. "Ani, are you in there?"

"I'm here," Ani says, waving the light so her mother can find her. While she listens for the tentative footsteps — her mother has always been afraid to walk alone in the dark — Ani closes her eyes and tries to re-imagine the way out.

Back when she stacked ice here, she forced herself to memorize the different turns in case the power was suddenly cut off and the lights went out, leaving her to find the door before becoming too cold. She practiced by tying a blindfold, a strip of old butcher's apron, around her eyes and feeling her way along the walls of meat lockers that customers rented to store their extra cuts of beef and pork. That way, if the freezer's motors droned to silence and the light withdrew into the walls, she would know what to do. But the day it finally happened, Ani was facing the wrong way. She became disoriented and lost her sense of direction. Reaching blindly into the space around her, Ani had scuffed along a few inches at a time, hesitation causing her to trip and her already frozen fingertips to bump into the solid hedges of wood.

From the time Ani turned nine, she lived with her mother and stepfather, Clive, in an apartment above the old red-bricked butcher shop with its deli in front. Before that she and her mother lived alone on Seventh Street in a small, blue-sided house with evergreen trees in front and a big backyard with a garden. Every spring, while Ani watched from a distance her grandfather decided was safe, he and one of her uncles drove down the back alley with a grain truck full of manure to spread on their garden. After they negotiated the truck into just the right position, by inching it back and forth in the narrow alley, they tilted the grain box until the manure began to spill over the back fence. Wearing rubber boots, they climbed inside and shovelled out the rest.

If it was a cool day, the garden steamed with the rich, composting fertilizer as the men tilled it into the soil with pitchforks. Afterwards Ani would hold the garden hose for them to wash their hands under, then go inside and carry out glasses of pink lemonade that tonkled with ice cubes, and plates of pink-frosted cream cookies her grandmother sent from the farm in an ice cream bucket.

"Sometimes a little shit is all a potato needs before it can grow," her grandfather said, pulling Ani onto his lap for a whisker rub as he sat on a sun-worsted lawn chair and they admired the garden together. Ani laughed behind her hands.

"Just don't repeat that to your father," her mother said later, trying not to laugh herself. "I have enough problems."

A few weeks after the manure was delivered, Ani's grandfather always came back into town to help them plant the peas and carrots, radishes, corn, potatoes, and the pale green kohlrabi Ani liked to eat raw and still warm from the sun. With an old, rusted hoe, he'd carve furrows into the soil and Ani would follow behind dropping seeds.

The butcher shop was downtown on Central Avenue, surrounded by parking lots and other stores on a one-way street where the traffic noise was constant. Upstairs, the apartment had windows on two sides, the south-facing ones overlooking a barely-used parking lot. From the east windows, Ani could watch the deliveries of freshly-slaughtered animals. Cows, pigs, lambs, and sometimes a deer, if a hunter wanted sausages made.

"You'll have a real papa now," Ani's grandfather said, reluctantly, as though he himself had only been a bookmark, keeping the place where a dad belonged. Her own father, who lived a province away in Edmonton, was too far away to fill the role more than a couple of times a year. Ani didn't see her grandfather as much after the wedding.

"Why can't you come live with us in *our* house?" Ani said to Clive one day, a few weeks before the ceremony. She and her mother had dropped by to visit him at work after buying new shoes to go with Ani's flower girl dress. Ani liked a pair of white sandals, but because the wedding was going to be in October — an unpredictable month for weather — Ani agreed to a pair of patent leather Mary Janes with embroidered butterflies on the toes.

"Come with me," he said and led Ani from the front of the shop, down the long, dark hallway towards the ice house, pushing aside a hanging pig carcass to let her by. "Hear that?" he said when they stopped in front of the big door that led inside the giant freezer.

"Uh huh," Ani said, although she didn't know what she was meant to listen to.

"I have to live here so I can tell if the motors in the ice house go off in the middle of the night. Otherwise I might come to work in the morning and find everything melted. Understand?" He opened the door and disappeared inside for a few moments before coming back out with a pair of popsicles. One for Ani and one to give to her mother.

At the time, although Ani knew the food in their freezer at home didn't thaw all that quickly during a power outage as long as the lid was left closed, she hadn't questioned Clive. And when she and her mother went home that day, she continued to quietly pack her things — plush animals into pillow cases; books and clothes into boxes and suitcases — and helped her mother throw away their old garden tools — the hoe and rake her grandfather had used, and the old kitchen utensils that Ani kept for making mud pies. They were too old and rusted to be of use to anyone else.

"You would have stopped playing with them soon, anyway," her mother said, as though it were a good thing. "Clive says his daughter, Caroline, used to spend all of her time painting with watercolours when she and her mother still lived with him."

Ani thought she'd like to meet Caroline. She imagined them painting together, going out to her grandparents' farm, Clive taking them for ice cream.

When Ani first met Clive, she was eight years old and it was the afternoon before she left to spend Christmas with her father's vegetarian family. Clive was a not-quite-tall man with black hair, and crinkles around his eyes that made him look as though he liked to laugh.

"Hey there, kiddo," he said, smiling so wide she could see his fillings. He put out his hand for Ani to shake. When she stepped forward to take it, his skin smelled smoky and warm, like bacon on Sunday mornings. Her mother later told her that he made his own bacon and sausages in his butcher shop.

"How'd you and your mom like to have Christmas dinner today?" Clive said. "Can't have you going without turkey this time of year now, can we?" He folded his arms across his chest and leaned back slightly in a way that made him look as though he knew all the best secrets.

"It's not Christmas yet," Ani said. She felt tingly, as though tiny bubbles were rising through her body, and knew this was what her father meant when he told her she was prone to reckless happiness — ready to give her heart away to anyone bringing presents.

"Just wait here a minute," Clive said.

Ani couldn't wait, and followed him into the winter air without a coat and mittens. The cold nipped at her fingers. In another month or so, the weather would become severe. In December though, it was still possible to rush outside and quickly back into the house before getting frostbitten.

While Ani danced back and forth to keep warm, Clive opened the trunk of his car — a large, square boat of a vehicle — and disappeared halfway inside. "Here, you can carry these," he said as he plopped a box full of brightly papered gifts into her arms. He reached back inside the trunk and came out with a plastic bin full of food and bottles of pink cream soda. On top he balanced an enormous turkey in a speckled black roasting pan. The turkey, its skin buttered and salted all over, wobbled in the pan. And carrying it, Clive looked like a character in a black-and-white movie — the kind that always finished with meaningful, cheery music that meant things had ended happily despite the possibility they might not have. The two of them laughed together when he nearly slipped, which would have sent the bird sledding down the icy sidewalk. For months afterwards, it was their inside joke. When Ani's mother told them she'd nearly fallen when the heel of her shoe broke, Ani would say, "At least you weren't carrying a turkey!"

The following October, wearing her new flower girl shoes and a soft-blue dress, Ani met Clive's daughter for the first time. He had picked up Caroline at the bus depot in the morning and taken her out for pancakes before driving her to the house on Seventh, where all the women and girls in the wedding party were getting ready to go to the church.

Caroline wasn't as Ani had imagined. She was neither shy nor friendly. Didn't have bouncy brunette curls and clothes that Ani could borrow. She didn't wear glasses, which Ani secretly wished they'd have in common. And, two years older, Caroline no longer played with dolls. When Ani asked her whether she had ordered blueberries on her pancakes, she rolled her eyes in a way that let Ani know she was exactly the way Caroline had expected her to be. A bumpkin with butterflies on her shoes.

"What does it matter?" she said. "It was just breakfast. Not like my dad hasn't taken me for pancakes before."

"I guess it doesn't matter," Ani said, drawing a curve in the carpet with the toe of her shoe. Until then, she had held a present for Caroline — a tiny silver heart on a chain that her mother helped her buy. Now she set it on her dresser next to a stack of moving boxes. Maybe someday when we're sisters, she thought. But later, although she looked everywhere, Ani couldn't find the necklace.

At the reception in the church basement, while Ani's mother surveyed the dessert table, and her uncles congratulated Clive, Ani wound her way through the chattering guests towards him. The guests were old ladies, mostly, who smelled like baby powder and wanted to pinch and kiss her cheeks. When she reached Clive, Ani slipped her hand into his, expecting his face to crinkle into a smile. She had been sure all day that he would want to give her something special, like at Christmas when he'd bought her a pair of hair combs studded with blue and green crystals and said they made her look as pretty as her mother. She had worn them every day for weeks, until one of the teeth broke and her mother said she should put them away.

"I'm happy you married my mom," she said and lowered her head shyly to look up at him through her bangs. "Dad."

Clive was quiet for a moment, his eyes skipping over her to where Caroline was holding a plate of fruitcake, distractedly pushing crumbs around with her finger. Ani watched him look at his daughter. He swallowed hard a few times.

"How are you and Caroline getting along?" he finally said.

"Okay. I mean, I think maybe she's tired from the bus." Ani tried to sound cheerful but wanted to tell him she didn't think Caroline wanted to be friends. While she tried to think of what else to say, he let go of her hand and turned away towards another conversation. Ani slipped through the guests and didn't see Clive again until he and her mother returned from their honeymoon in Saskatoon.

When they came home early one morning, Ani and the aunt who had stayed with her met them at the door. Clive's face creased but he didn't smile the way he used to. He handed her a gold-coloured pen with a digital clock beside the pocket clip, the kind of pen a salesman might carry.

"He just doesn't know what girls your age like," her mother said quietly when he had left the room. Ani thought of the hair combs and knew it wasn't true. "I didn't want to discourage him by saying so. Maybe you can go thank him, and then you and I can run out to the Dairy Queen later to get treats for all of us."

That same day Ani and her mother moved into Clive's apartment. Ani's new bedroom had red carpeting and, after a few days, pink-painted walls. She and her mother had gone to the hardware store across the street together and picked out the colour. They rolled it over the existing wallpaper while Clive was downstairs at the butcher shop. The paint covered up the colours in the paper, but hadn't been able to disguise the little embossed girls carrying baskets of flowers. They were still there as shadows in the paint.

Later, while Ani's mother was shopping for supper, Clive came upstairs and found Ani sitting in her room, admiring the fresh pink.

"Caroline chose that wallpaper," Clive said slowly. He crossed his arms. "I put it up for her. Damn it, kid." He turned his back to her and left the room. He closed the door behind him, tightly. An hour later, Ani still didn't know whether she should come out.

After supper though, Ani found Clive looking through the pages of his family picture albums. She went into her room, dug through a box and found one of her own. She brought it to the living room and sat next to Clive on the couch.

In her stepfather's pictures, Caroline was often seen dabbing a paintbrush on a canvas in the room that used to be hers and was clean and tidy for every picture. Ani's pictures were mostly of her in rubber boots, tromping through her grandfather's barn, or in the kitchen with a careless mess of flour and batter spilled on the counter.

"I'm sorry," Ani said, although she still didn't understand why he was so upset with her.

Clive pointed to a picture of Caroline in which nothing around her was out of place. "I think we'll make putting things away a rule around here, eh, kiddo?" He clapped her on the shoulder, as though they'd thought of a good plan together. "Everyone does their part so the place doesn't go to hell in our sleep?" He laughed and Ani tried to laugh, too, as if there was something funny about what he'd said. Afterwards, she took her photo album back to her room.

A few days later Ani came home from school to find her favourite doll, Susie, stuffed in the kitchen garbage and Clive sitting across at the table. He'd been waiting for her.

"Why do you think I did that?" he said.

Ani licked her lips and pressed them together. Blood was rushing through her ears.

"I don't know," she said.

"Where did you leave it this morning?"

"In the kitchen? Next to my cereal bowl?" It was a guess, but she hoped if she guessed right, he'd let her have her doll back.

"Right. You left the bowl for your mother or me to clean up, and you and I both know that you know better than that."

"But, she — " Ani gestured at the doll, its dress already dirtied with potato peelings and wet coffee grounds. Ani longed to rescue her, wash her up and put her back in her room. She'd promise to never leave her lying around again.

"You're getting too old for dolls, anyway," Clive said. He stood up and patted Ani, in a reassuring way, on the shoulder before pushing the lid down on top of the garbage. "Now don't let me see you trying to get that thing out of there."

Later, when Ani's mother found her crying on her bed, Ani tried to explain what had happened. But it came out sounding childish.

"Susie will think I let her get thrown out." Ani said. "She won't understand."

Ani buried her head in her knees and sobbed. The next day was garbage day, and she felt sick to her stomach imagining what would happen to her doll. Susie would be covered in other people's garbage and compressed before being taken to the nuisance grounds.

"I'm sorry, but there's nothing we can do about it now, honey. That was one of Clive's rules," her mother said. "Maybe we'll both have to be more careful and considerate." She squeezed Ani into a hug. "I'm sure he didn't intend to be mean. Just remember how well the two of you got along last Christmas."

Ani could no longer sleep. Clive insisted she become accustomed to noise at night, and to light from the television that flickered from the living room to the frenetic rhythm of old western shoot-outs. And if it wasn't the TV, the scratchy sounds of old country and western records whined in her ears. Even after Clive finally turned them off and he and her mother went to bed, the motors from the ice house droned on and off all night. They flicked a switch in her mind every time they powered up.

"It's something you're just going to have to get used to," Clive told her the first time she crept out of her room and asked if he could turn down the record player.

"Just a little?" She looked to her mother, who was reading a magazine. "I can't get to sleep."

"Well, it won't happen with you standing here. Just put it out of your mind," Clive said.

Ani wanted to tell him that it was stupid to think anyone could sleep through all that horrible honky-tonk. Although the words were climbing up her throat, she didn't let them out. After she went back to bed, she heard her mother and Clive talking.

"It's not her fault," her mother said. "I always made sure it was quiet for her at night."

"Sure you did, and now she expects it. You didn't do her any favours by spoiling her, you know."

"I just think it's a lot to adjust to — a new home along with everything else."

Clive disagreed and that was the end of it.

By the time Ani was ten, a year after her mother married Clive, it became harder and harder at school to hide her fatigue. After math one day, her teacher, Mr. Buchanan, told her to stay in her seat. When all the other students were gone, he came and leaned over her.

"I'd like to know why you're always so tired in my class, Ani," he said. "Do you have a proper bed time?"

Ani was quiet and didn't look at him, but she could feel pressure building in her chest as though her heart was a balloon, ready to burst.

"Do you have an answer for me?" Mr. Buchanan said.

Still looking down, Ani said the only thing she knew that would get him off her case. "It's just PMS." She got up out of her desk and left the room. After that, Mr. Buchanan left her alone, and Ani knew it was because ever since Janelle Klassen had gotten her period when she was nine and a half, and told him so, he let her get out of anything she wanted. "Can I sit out of gym class because I have cramps?" became Janelle's favourite way to be excused from a hated sport. Mr. Buchanan's face would turn beet red and he'd let her get away with anything.

There were times over those first years when Ani thought Clive was finally getting used to having her around, that he might decide to like her again. He took her fishing once, but when Ani couldn't think of what to talk about between casting her line, he told her she didn't know how to appreciate anything and if she wasn't careful she was going to become a gloomy girl. "Nobody likes gloomy girls."

"Yeah, well nobody likes being called gloomy, either," Ani said. It was the first time she had ever answered him that way. Afterwards, she began to avoid Clive whenever possible. A hard thing to do in an apartment.

One morning he came upstairs from the butcher shop and found Ani brushing her hair in front of the bathroom mirror, getting ready for the first day of the seventh grade. He stopped in front of the door and stepped into the bathroom behind her. He stared at Ani's reflection until she was forced to look back at him.

"I'm going to give you some advice," he said. "My life hasn't always been a hayride, but every morning I look at myself in the mirror and grin or make a funny face. I decide to be happy and that's that."

Ani rolled her eyes. "You've got to be kidding."

"You know what your problem is, right? You take yourself too seriously. Just try it once."

"This is dumb," she said. But when he didn't leave, she stuck her tongue out at herself.

"You can do better than that. Try again."

Ani studied her own face, her forehead that was breaking out in a fresh crop of pimples, the dark circles under her eyes. She stuck out her tongue again and looked at Clive in the mirror to see if their little exercise was over and she could go.

"Again," he said.

But when Ani forced her face into a smile, it was like drawing electricity from a pickle — an experiment from her sixth grade science class. It didn't last, and you had to use a different pickle every time.

"I'm going to be late," she said.

"Never mind that. Watch." Clive said and his face crinkled, his eyes lighting up as though the movement of his mouth had turned on a bulb. The twinkle Ani still remembered from when she first knew him appeared. But now she knew it was nothing more than a bare bulb in an empty room, and the switch could be turned off without warning.

Nevertheless, for weeks afterwards, Ani forced herself to look happy around Clive, even though it made her feel fake. She spread an artificial smile across her face when he gave her the job of packing ice after school.

She wore the smile as she shoved her arm, shoulder deep into the ice machines with an aluminum scoop, piled the cubes into plastic bags printed with cartoon polar bears and loaded them into the grocer's cart.

She didn't show on her face when her fingers froze, became clumsy and slipped off the handle into the sharp ice that cut her skin. Just little nicks, like paper cuts, but when there were enough of them, they stung like crazy.

Most of the time Ani worked as fast as she could so she'd only have to make one trip into the back. It was hard to keep the first bags she'd filled from melting before she could finish tying up the last. But she dreaded pushing the loaded cart down the narrow hallway because along the way hung the carcasses of pigs brought in through the back door. Suspended from a track in the ceiling by hooks slipped between the bones and tendons of their hind feet, the pigs were heavy and stiff, hard to push aside to make room for the cart. No matter how many times she did it, she never got used to their raw, porky smell, or having to touch their lardy hides with her bare hands.

One day, as she pushed the cart into the hallway and began to make her way past the first carcass, she nearly bumped into Clive coming from the smoke house.

"Hey there, kiddo," he said, looking at the way she was touching a pig with just the tips of her fingers. She gave the carcass, with its scooped-out belly and bristly pink skin, a big shove to show that it didn't bother her.

"I have to get these bags into the ice house before they melt," she said, hoping Clive would let her go on her way without saying anything else.

"You've let most of it melt already." He wiped his bloodied hands on the front of his apron and blocked Ani's way. Ani stood up a little straighter, although she wished she could back down and leave. She wished, also, that her mother, who was busy with customers at the front of the shop, would come and interrupt them. Clive was careful around her, though, and if he did say something mean, he did it in a joking way that could be mistaken for being friendly. In fact, half of the time Ani couldn't tell, either.

"You know, Caroline used to do your job, and she was happy to help out," he said. "She didn't think she was too good to do it."

"As long as I pack the ice, does it matter if I'm happy about it?" she said, holding his gaze.

ICE HOUSE

"Well, I guess that's the difference between you two. She didn't mind getting her hands a little dirty. You could learn a thing or two from her." He took one of Ani's hands and rubbed the blood from his own hands into it, mashing gritty bits of fat between her fingers.

Ani stiffened. When she spoke, her voice wavered.

"Can I ask you something?" Ani said. Whatever courage she had a moment ago had already drained away, but she went on anyway. "Wouldn't the ice house stay frozen even if the power went out? Even if it was left overnight? There was no reason we had to come live here, was there? You just didn't want to change anything for me."

"You think you have everything all figured out, don't you?" Clive said. He grinned and his eyes crinkled at the corners, as though they were playing a game and Ani had just made a bad move.

Ani gave the cart a push and Clive let her pass. In a few moments she opened the door to the ice house and disappeared inside. She breathed in the cold, crisp air until she felt calmer. Unlike in the rest of the shop, where the smell of meat was heavy and sickening, here the smells were absorbed in the ice.

Despite the cold, Ani worked slowly at stacking the bags she'd packed, laying down a row and placing the next bags on top in the grooves in between. Her mother always said she was proud of Ani's neat rows. It was, Ani thought, a silly thing to be proud of.

With the last bag in place, Ani was about to turn the cart around and push it back through the alleys of lockers towards the door, when the lights went out. There was a moment before it became completely dark. The light seemed suspended, as though taking a breath. Then it was gone. And it was quiet.

Ani heard her heartbeat quicken, her clothes rasp as she turned suddenly and bumped into the cart.

When she reached out to find something to hold onto, the tips of her frost-burnt fingers bumped into the nearest wall of meat lockers. Blindly, she touched the wood, fingering the hinges and locks that were pitted with rust. As Ani felt her way in the direction she thought the door was, she began to shiver. She tried to focus on her hands moving along the lockers, placing her feet one in front of the other. Except for what she could touch, the room had disappeared, and so had her memory of how to find the way out. Blood beat against her eardrums as she groped along the lockers and came to a dead end in the maze. There, she pressed her back into the wall and hung her head. She slid down to sit on her heels, feeling icy, metal latches scrape through her clothes and cut her skin. She listened to the silence, focused on the darkness.

Now, ten years later, the ice house's motors have gone silent for good. Not even the drone of outside traffic penetrates the thick layers of insulation.

"Ani," her mother says, startling her. For a moment, Ani is still that young girl. She's trapped and her mother has finally come to find her and show her the way out. She shivers, then remembers that the room is uncomfortably warm and the entire building will soon be torn down.

"What were you thinking about just now?" her mother says, but doesn't leave a space for Ani to answer. "You have to come have a look at what I found up front."

"I got lost in here once. The lights went off," Ani says.

For a moment her mother looks startled. Her voice is forcibly bright. "No, I don't think so, honey. I would have known about that. Or Clive would have known and said something. One of us would have found you. Your stepfather always sensed when something was wrong." She takes Ani's hand and holds it tightly, but doesn't look at her. Then she turns around and walks away, leaving Ani to follow her out of the ice house to the front of the shop.

When the lights finally came back on that day in the ice house, Ani tried to get up and run to the door. She had no reason to think her mother would be there waiting for her on the other side, but was sure of it, anyway.

Ani was too cold to run, and stumbled clumsily, using the lockers for balance. When she got to the door, she threw it open and plunged into the hallway. Her lungs stung with the warm air.

But instead of her mother, she tripped into one of the pigs hanging from the ceiling and set it dancing like a grotesque ballerina. She fell backwards onto the cement floor. Ani was sure there hadn't been a pig that close to the door when she went in.

"I got lost in there once," Ani says to herself. She knows if her mother doesn't believe she was ever trapped, she would never believe that when Ani looked up from where she fell, she saw Clive there, his arms folded, watching her.

"Did it start to thaw in there?" he asked.

"Look. See, it's as though he left it for you," Ani's mother says when Ani catches up with her at the front of the shop. Her voice is high and hopeful as she reaches into the glass-fronted deli showcase, stinking now of rancid fat and ancient cheese. She takes out a glass bottle.

"Strawberry cream soda," her mother says, although the candy-pink liquid doesn't need explanation. After that first Christmas, before Clive married her mother, he used to buy them for Ani. Before, but not after. "Clive knew it was your favourite. Take it. It's still good."

"It smells like old meat," Ani says.

"That's just on the outside. Here, we'll wash it up at home. We have a bottle opener. Maybe you and Clive can share it, for old times or something."

"Mom, please listen to me. I don't want it."

"Oh, well, I'll carry it for you, then." She slips the bottle into her purse.

"I guess we never thought this place would be torn down, did we?" Ani's mother says, although it's not really a question. "I know your stepfather certainly didn't. He thought our grandchildren would visit us here. All of our grandchildren, not just Caroline's children."

"It's not much of a place for kids," Ani says.

"No, maybe not."

"The dead pigs were pretty creepy," Ani says with a little laugh. There had also been cows, headless lambs with wool socks and, once, a calf's heart that Ani found on the butchering table next to the saws and grinders, still faintly beating where Clive left it.

Both curious and repelled, Ani reached out to touch the purple, fatted muscle. The heart had latched onto Ani's hand, startling her. She wanted to pull her hand back, but her finger slipped into the aorta and the heart suckled it for a few desperate gulps before it finally fell still.

For what seemed like a long time, Ani stood there, unable to pull away. Until Clive found her and said, "Those things'll latch onto anything."

Ani regrets coming for this last look around the old butcher shop with her mother. At first it had seemed like the right thing to do, like visiting a relative in hospital, making peace before they pull the plug.

"You should come see inside the place one more time, don't you think?" her mother had suggested on the phone, pleased when Ani agreed. "And tell that fiancé of yours to come, too. Before you two get married, he should see where you grew up."

When it came time, Ani had left Joshua at her mother and Clive's rented house, afraid he wouldn't be able to see beyond the butcher shop's now-empty rooms. That what had taken place in them would be invisible to him, like it was to the customers who'd once stood on the other side of the meat case, waiting their turn to be served. They preferred to think the steaks and roasts, the smoked and processed meats they took home in neat paper packages, hadn't been cut from the carcasses of dead animals dangling out of sight in the back hall.

"I think we'll have a look upstairs, too, won't we," Ani's mother asks, seeming disappointed that the cream soda was not the find she expected it to be. "I'm sure you want to have a look at your old room again before it's gone."

Together they climb the creaking wooden stairs attached to the outside of the building and let themselves into the apartment with their old key, which still works in the lock.

"It hasn't changed," Ani says when they step inside.

"Did Clive tell you people from town are asking about the old bricks once the building comes down? They want them for fireplaces. It's a nice idea, don't you think?" She waits for Ani to agree.

"I don't know. It seems strange, I guess."

"Well, I think it makes Clive feel better to know that parts of the old place will live on. It might even be nice if you and Joshua ask him to put some aside for you. For when you build your own home."

"Mom. Really. You should know there's nothing here I want to take with me," Ani says.

"Oh, I don't know about that," she says, leading Ani into her old bedroom — Caroline's old bedroom.

"We must have had some happy times here together though, didn't we? I hope you haven't told Joshua that there was nothing good about living here."

"I haven't said much of anything," Ani says.

"Well, I hope you told him about that Christmas before we were married, how Clive came over to our house with that silly turkey that you two laughed over for weeks afterwards. Honestly, I don't know what happened to you two later on. You seemed to get along so well, and suddenly you became so cold towards him. Why was that?"

"It wasn't sudden, Mom," Ani says, feeling tired. The sound of the ice house's motors has followed her to college and she still doesn't sleep well at night.

"Well, whatever it was, I know Clive was always sorry you two weren't closer. Especially after you seemed happy about us becoming a family."

"It didn't turn out the way I expected."

"Well," her mother says. She's biting her lip and looking down at her feet. "I guess we don't always get what we thought, but sometimes we still get what we asked for."

Ani is quiet for what seems like a long time. She reaches for a strip of the painted-over wallpaper that has begun to peel away from the wall.

"I didn't ask for this," she says and hands her mother the paper. "This was Caroline's wallpaper, her room. It was never mine."

"Of course it was yours. And I had to cook in his wife's kitchen and sleep in her bed. But I made them mine." She turns away from Ani and walks into a corner, and Ani suddenly understands that her mother's been backed into one all these years. In one hand her mother is holding the piece of wallpaper. Her other hand is empty.

Ani looks at her mother and shakes her head.

"Maybe we should pick up a treat for all of us on the way home," Ani says, stepping aside to let her mother by.

Her mother is quiet for a moment. "What a nice idea," she says and gives the strip of torn wallpaper back to Ani.

Little Lamb

My brother may seem stupid. But really, Henry is just young.
Not too young to know certain things, mind you. Like that we're
Mennonite. Which of course means we understand that farming
and inventing new ways to be backwards is the only sure way into
grace. For example, we're the last farm within a hundred miles to
go without a flush toilet, and that makes us makes us little closer
to Heaven than any of our neighbours.

That's the easy stuff to understand. The kind you just know
because you're born to it and it's talked about all the time, at
breakfast, dinner, and supper and every moment that it can be
crammed in between. Then there's the stuff a kid can't know until
he's learned it for himself.

Take, for example, the Sears catalogue. It's Dad's until he gives
it to Mom. She tears out pages with pictures of practical things
and saves them in case she's allowed to make an order. And when
she isn't, she uses them to line the kitchen drawers. That way, to
get rid of all the mouse droppings that collect there overnight, all
a kid has to do is crumple up the liner.

Usually the pages in the drawers picture things like grey wool
socks, like the ones that get shredded inside our field boots by a
mealy mixture of shattered hay and mud, churned with sweat that

turns to mortar. A sock can still be saved if you know how to work a darning needle. So there's no cause to be hasty ordering fresh ones.

On the other hand, a new pair every other Christmas would be swell.

Dad tears out all the pages with dirty pictures, too; the ones with women in bras and girdles. I know he does this because he thinks we'll sin with them while doing our business in the old outshed. As though anyone would want to be in that damp, creaky, reeking upright coffin a half-second longer than we have to.

After Mom and Dad have had their way with the catalogue, then it's ours, and what's left is a picture book of things we can't have. Things Dad doesn't think any kids of his could ever want. He's too thick between the ears to know that those are the pages that tempt us the most. Henry is only eight years old and he couldn't care less about women's torsos in white cotton scaffolding. The only women he knows are Mom and the one-and-only teacher at our dumb country school, and neither of them have anything under their dresses that any of us want to see.

When we got the last winter catalogue, reminding us that it was now 1954 in the parts of the world that weren't Mennonite country, Henry was bent on getting a sled. Pretty unoriginal of him, if you ask me, since each of us boys wanted one at one time or another. When it was me, I even offered to do extra chores. I got the chores, all right. But never saw a sled. Lesson learned.

Henry figured it out too, when in place of a sled he inherited a pair of ice skates with the slackest boot leather you've ever seen. They'd already been worn by three cousins and our other two brothers. With no support, his ankles fells inwards and ached. It was colder than a witch's tit that day, too (I learned that saying at recess from Erich Wiens, who everyone knows is going straight to hell). When my brother tried to skate on the frozen slough that he trudged a whole mile from the house to get to, the ice was too cold to melt under the blunt blades and all he managed to do was shuffle from end to end, his feet growing cold, then dangerously hot, then numb. He had to walk all the way home in the deep snow and by the time he got back was howling like we'd stuck him in the meat grinder. He blubbered even more when Mom dunked his feet in a bowl of warm water and rubbed his toes, which had gone white. But he stopped pretty quick when Dad came in and gave him the biggest bawling out of his life for being such a little wiener. None of his toes even fell off.

After that Henry didn't want to play outside at all and it no longer mattered that he didn't have a sled. He tore out the page with its picture, crammed it in his pocket, and snuck it into the outhouse with him. Exactly the way Dad worried we would if he slipped up and gave us a chance to go in there with the girdled ladies.

Of course I didn't see what Henry did in there, but I know. Same thing I did with a picture of a hockey stick once: crumpled the paper to soften it a little before sending it to a more fitting end.

Unlike the rest of the chores we have to do, Henry actually enjoys shovelling out the concrete shit-trenches after the cows have been milked. He replaces their soiled bedding with new hay. And I'll give it to him that it really is the better of the chores in any season. Although it's also a trap.

Henry's always been soft towards all the newborn animals on the farm, whether they're meant for the slaughterhouse or not. Calves and chicks. Mangy puppies. Even the mice we poison and the gophers we bury alive in their holes.

Dad say there's no place on a farm for softness.

Yet, ever since the birth of a late lamb this year, Henry has stolen time from kneeling on the concrete floor in our basement bedroom and repenting of his sinful nature. Instead, he hurries through mucking out the rest of the barn and leaves the lamb's stall to the last.

I know Henry thinks I'm just like Dad. But I know the chilling warmth Henry feels when the lamb sucks on his fingers, eager for salt. I know, too, how my brother slides down to sit on his heels to watch the lamb as it plays, all innocent and forgetful that it's just living meat.

They're all the same, lambs. Sure, every animal born on the farm is cute and whatever, until they get the axe or, like unwanted kittens, drowned in the rain barrel. A lamb's only hope is if it grows up, produces some offspring of its own — before it gets the hatchet.

Henry's lamb is no exception. It has spindly, elastic legs and is all pathetically adorable when it bounds around the stall, or nips at its mother's tail, or climbs up her shifting mound of wool. Henry laughs when it does that. He pinches his nose to keep quiet as the lamb teeters onto its mother's head and either falls or jumps into the fresh nest of hay. It nurses, then sleeps, and Henry comes to the house for supper at exactly five o'clock.

But Henry has made a mistake today. He didn't show up for supper. And although it was only a matter of time until he slipped up, now he'll have to learn that mistakes never go unrewarded around here.

I'm the first to find him in the lamb's stall. He doesn't wake up until I roughly rock him with my boot. "Hey, Mary, wake up."

Henry asks what time it is and I tell him that "It's after supper. Mom's worried sick and Dad's sick of her worrying." (That's something Dad would say.) "He wouldn't let us look for you until we all cleaned off our plates."

You'd think we'd be hungry and grateful and want to finish our supper after all the slave labour we do, but none of us have wanted to eat our mother's cooking since Dad hit the oldest, gnarliest, pronghorn deer on the whole damn planet with the truck and brought it home. I don't know what part we ate tonight, but I think there's a butthole stuck in my throat.

"Is he mad?" Henry says, rubbing his eyes with his fists like a little girl.

"Are you an idiot"? I ask, adding grit.

He wants to cry, I can tell he does. He's thinking about throwing sheep dung at me and I wish he would. But the ringing of Dad's boots clomping across the floor of the barn quickly snuffs Henry's courage.

Stand up. Don't look up, I think, as intensely as I can.

He stays down, with his legs folded behind him. He's holding the lamb's ear between his thumb and fingers, stroking it like a baby blanket. If anyone's asking for a beating, that's exactly how to do it.

He looks up and I think, Don't look down.

He looks down. He knows he's in trouble, but doesn't get what he's done wrong.

I know his muscles will be hurting him by now from cold that's crept up through the floor into his legs. Dad stands over him, glowering long enough to make him really feel it, and then a little longer, for good measure.

"You come find me when you have something to tell me," Dad says. He never says what we should come tell him. We have to figure that bit out for ourselves.

Before he leaves, Dad spits on the floor, as though spitting the taste of fatherhood out of his mouth. Henry looks at me when he's gone and I call him a little shit. I mean it to help toughen him because scar tissue is tougher than regular skin. Henry needs to learn that Dad doesn't have any soft edges. He cherishes his anger, keeps it clenched like a closed fist around a sharp pebble until the stone has created a scar. He has a collection of these souvenirs, gained from teaching each of his sons a lesson.

By the next morning Dad's breathing is coarse enough to scour Henry's shame, which he's carried through the night, to a fine polish. I can practically see myself in its reflection.

It's a school day today and we're already late and waiting to be dismissed from the table. If we have to run to be on time, the breakfast that's lumping in our guts will turn to cement.

"We have to go. Teacher will be upset with us," Henry says, a feeble attempt to save the rest of us. We use the distraction and leave him as a sacrifice. It's him Dad wants, anyway.

"You go too," Mom says to him before we're all out the door. Then, to Dad, "He'll be late and Mrs. Knelson will think we have trouble at home."

"Go on," she says to Henry.

Momma's boy.

"You're too damn attached to that lamb," Dad says, unable to deny his wife's good sense. It's a parting shot that hits its target squarely between the shoulders before Henry limps away.

Outside, the lamb is in the barnyard with its mother, separate from the other sheep. Henry stops to pet it and says, "Don't worry." When it pushes its nose into his hand, he promises to be back soon. You can see that the affection makes my brother hurt. The way he walks away from the lamb, I can tell he's already learning.

I can tell, too, that Henry is nervous. He hums while he walks, fitting notes together like a puzzle with no solution. He begins to tug on a frayed thread on the cuff of his sweater until it becomes a hole, its fibres reaching out to one another across the damage. He falls way behind by the time we've walked the two miles to school, and the next time I see him is through the classroom window when he nearly goes past the school.

He slinks through the door and into the back of the class. He's trying to be very small. It only makes him more visible.

Later, when school is let out, we start by walking home with him. He's slow and mopey, and soon we leave him behind to find his own way. Before we're too far ahead we turn back and bleat, "Baa." We feel sly. Slick. Smart.

Henry absorbs our taunt and continues to shuffle, looking as though he's been shot full of lead. We're doing him a kindness. He's about to find out whether he has enough scar tissue to protect him.

We're the first onto the yard and so we're the first to see. We walk by, all of us, and look right at it. It's the only way Dad will let us keep going.

None of us can run back and help Henry now. He's too close and looking down at his feet, one shoelace trailing through the dust and tripping him.

"Keep going," I say under my breath. But he looks up and stops.

There's Dad, sharpening the knife he uses for killing.

There's the lamb, tied to the fence. Henry looks at Dad and Dad holds out the knife.

"Don't cry," I say quietly. He doesn't.

"Don't look away." He doesn't.

MENNONITES DON'T DANCE

LIZBETH BENT TO PICK UP A spoon, wiped away the small splat of cream gravy left where it had fallen, and paused to watch her mother and sisters' feet moving over the kitchen floor. A choreography of sensible shoes.

If she'd had her way, Lizbeth would've hitched a ride into town that morning with her father and two of her brothers. Even though all they planned to do there was buy two more cartons of grapefruit and maybe argue down the price of a reconditioned tractor.

Lizbeth would've given her left braid to get near a little civilization, even if it was only Swift Current. From the tractor yard she could watch people as they walked along the sidewalk. Imagine they were going to the mall or a matinée. More than anything, Lizbeth wanted to go to a matinée.

She was a bother in the kitchen, anyway. But because hundreds of years of Mennonite tradition weren't about to give her a day off to indulge in some civilization, she swaddled herself in an apron first thing every morning, just like her mother and sisters. Sisters who, unlike Lizbeth, never thought of running to the edge of their village to see whether they'd fall off a precipice. Straight into the real world.

Since she couldn't go into the city accompanied by at least one member of her family, the best part of Lizbeth's day, the part she lived for, was when her father and brothers came in from the fields for lunch. Lizbeth plonked whatever bowl of dough she was babysitting onto the counter and hurried to meet them at the door.

Her oldest brother, Matthew — who lived three houses down the one-and-only road in the village, and had already spent ten years getting his own house ready for the wife God had pre-planned for him, whoever she was — was the first one in the door. He chuckled at Lizbeth, greeting him at the door as faithfully as any dog, and set down a bulging crate of citrus. "Been doing lots of cooking, I see."

No one in the family could miss the fact that their mother's domestic genes had been magnetically repelled by Lizbeth. No one took it very seriously. They all assumed Lizbeth would eventually fit into the mould.

She already belonged in other ways, though. Her thighs, for example, which had thickened since she turned thirteen, certainly made her look Mennonite.

Matthew tousled Lizbeth's hair, although she was old enough that he'd soon have to stop kidding with her. Just one more reason, as far as Lizbeth could tell, that there was nothing much to look forward to about growing up. Especially growing up Mennonite. The only people more excruciatingly bland were the Hutterites, with their farm cooperatives and shared everything. Like living in a nunnery, except you still had to clean up after the men and have dozens and dozens of children.

Lizbeth's mother had grown up a Hutterite. Since they came from the same square wheel as the Mennos, her marriage to Lizbeth's father didn't make them unequally yoked. It explained a lot, though. Like why her mother alternately defended communal living, yet was glad to be among Mennonites and all their loosey-goosey ways.

"The Hutterites have the best sewing machines you'll ever see," Lizbeth's mother told her once, as though it were an object lesson. A little memory nugget Lizbeth could keep in her pocket. Same as, "You won't want to be caught with idle hands if the Lord returns today."

"So, what's the point of a fancy sewing machine if you think zippers are the Devil's fastener?" Lizbeth had retorted.

"That's the Amish, honey," her mother said, as though that made Mennonites, who had shunned rubber tires for years, normal. Lizbeth considered it a modern miracle that her family owned two Ford trucks and a car. One of the trucks was Matthew's. And the car was for taking Lizbeth's mother wherever she needed to go, which was usually to the church with a jellied salad. She had an entire cookbook of jellied salads, and never made the same one twice.

The first four of Lizbeth's brothers were named for the Gospels, and the youngest of all the Klassen kids for the Apostle Paul, which had made Sunday school memorizations easy for Lizbeth for about a minute, until they moved on to the disciples and books of the Old Testament. There were also Mary, Ruth and Lizbeth; not quite Elizabeth.

"Hey, where's John?" Lizbeth asked when all of her other brothers and father had filed into the house for lunch. She weaved her way around them and leaned out the door, anxious to see her favourite brother, older than her by only two years.

When Lizbeth had had trouble writing a school essay on the differences between the first four books of the New Testament, and why they didn't contradict each other, John was the one who stayed up with her late into the night, until she could explain it to him backwards and forwards. She'd wanted to write about the differences between her brothers: "How Matthew, Mark, Luke and John (and Paul) All Have Separate Arms and Legs but Share the Same Brain." John had laughed, but hadn't let her write it, saying it was important to understand why the Bible made sense.

"He went to the barn," said Matthew, tossing the words over his shoulder like salt. He'd already pressed a slice of cold butter into a fresh bun and was about to reach for another. "Said he wanted to check on that old cow that's about ready to drop its calf."

"Mom. Can I take him his lunch?" Lizbeth said as her mother hurried over to the table with a plate of chicken, another of cold ham and hot, boiled wieners.

"Yes, yes, go. Take enough for you both," she said. "Just put on some rubber overshoes first." Lizbeth grabbed a handful of buns, forked some meat into them, and snatched both of the chicken's feet before her mother finally swished her away with the same distracted affection as when she whisked cats from the front door with a broom.

With her bundle of food and a thermos of strong coffee, Lizbeth hurried over the gravel path from the house to the barn. After all those hours in the kitchen, she was relieved to be outside and running. Every few steps though, she had to slow down and rearrange her hurriedly assembled picnic, as well as the long skirt of her housedress that kept bunching up between her legs.

She didn't even care. Not when, all morning, she'd plotted how to get out of the kitchen. And, now that she'd unexpectedly been given a reprieve, Lizbeth put a tick into her column of prayers God had answered. If she was lucky she might even have time to show John the new game she'd thought of, using empty coffee tins and a quarter she found on the way home from school. Whoever won would get to keep the quarter.

"C'mon Lizzy, help me with her," John said when Lizbeth swung open the barn door. His back was to her but he didn't need to turn around to see who was there. He always knew it was her.

"Just a sec." Lizbeth stepped into the milk-separating room, which smelled of sour milk but was kept as clean as her mother's dish cupboard.

Lizbeth set down the food on a scrubbed melamine table in the centre of the room and joined John at of the calving stall.

"She's in trouble," he said when Lizbeth came up behind him. The Jersey lay on its side, barely moving. Lizbeth recognized the animal as the oldest cow of their family's modest herd, the one that Lizbeth liked best because it didn't swish its tail in her face when milked, even though it was known for doing it to everyone else. "I don't know that we can save her, but the calf maybe."

"I brought lunch," Lizbeth said. The boys were always starved by noon and John, at almost sixteen, had the biggest appetite of them all. He usually wolfed down his food and looked around to see if anyone had leftovers. Their mother was as proud of John's appetite as any godly woman could afford to be. She liked to tell her fellow church ladies, as they sat around quilting or filling boxes for orphanages in Paraguay, that he ate a loaf of bread every day. "Sure, Mom. It's a real triumph." Lizbeth had snorted as she stuffed some New Testament finger puppets into the orphan boxes, although she thought everything about John was pretty cool. Even the fact that he wasn't very cool was cool to her.

"Later. We have to deliver this calf right now," John said, snapping Lizbeth back to the present.

"We?" said Lizbeth. "I can go back to the house. I can run there. Dad or Matthew — "

"Nuh-uh, this old girl's always liked you," John said. He grabbed her hand and tugged her towards the cow. "She'll be better if you're here. Help me get her up." He nudged Lizbeth round to the front of the animal.

Lizbeth nervously tucked her skirt between her legs, wishing she'd snuck on a pair of Paul's trousers under her dress. Slipping her hands beneath the cow's shoulder, she saw something move under the taut drum of its distended belly. The calf must still be alive. Lizbeth was as glad for her brother's sake as anything. He was always the one to get attached to the livestock, as though they weren't all destined for the sausage grinder sooner or later.

"Okay, now," John said, and together they started to rock the cow, trying to give her enough momentum to get to her feet. If she couldn't, they'd have to call their father to come with the tractor and chains.

"Good girl, you're okay." Lizbeth murmured encouragingly, bending down until she leaned her whole body into the bulk of the animal, her face pressed against its warm hide. "Just get up and it will all be okay. Please," she said and began to pray. Please, it's just another cow, but it will make my brother happy. Oh, and also because cows cost money, she added, thinking of what a waste it would be if her father lost a cow and a calf on the same day. Anyway, it seemed like the right thing to pray, more persuasive than if she asked something for herself.

With an urgent lowing sound that reminded Lizbeth of the way she herself moaned when she had the stomach flu and was about to be sick, the cow got to its knees. It laboured to breathe, it's ribs working like bellows, until it finally managed to stand.

"There now," Lizbeth said, pleased that her prayer appeared to be working. She stroked the broad plane between the cow's eyes. From where Lizbeth stood, she could see her brother work. He unbuttoned his sleeve cuff and pushed it up to his shoulder before he plunged his arm deep inside the backend of the cow. Lizbeth cringed, unsure whether she should feel worse for the cow or John.

"Keep her still," he said. And after a few minutes, "Okay, come and see this, Lizzy."

Lizbeth brushed her hand along the side of the cow as she walked, to let it know where she was, and came round to stand next to her brother in a puddle of water and blood and liquid black manure that smelled worse than anything Lizbeth had ever smelled. She wished she had obeyed her mother and put on the overshoes.

John was covered in a wash of mucousy red fluid that soaked through his clothes and dripped like snot onto his rubber boots. He had smeared it across the side of his face when he'd withdrawn his arm from the cow. Probably the only things left clean are his socks, Lizbeth thought, knowing his clothes wouldn't even make it into today's laundry. She tried not to imagine what they'd smell like after being stuffed into the hamper and left to ripen and get crusty for a day or two.

This wasn't the first time Lizbeth had seen calving and she thought she knew what to expect. Still, she'd never been right up to the business end of things. A spindly leg emerged, before withdrawing again, as though testing the air to see whether it was a nice day outside. Another leg, followed by a brown nose, already snuffling. John spread a bed of fresh straw before he slipped his hand past the small brown head and carefully guided the calf out of its mother, until the entire little animal spilled onto the straw and the mother crumpled back onto her side.

"What will happen to the calf if the mother dies?" Lizbeth said as she helped her brother rub the newborn down with fresh handfuls of hay.

"He'll be fine so long as one of the other cows cares for him. Otherwise, I guess you and I will have to take turns giving him milk from a bucket."

At the old water pump next to the house, Lizbeth and John stopped to wash up before eating the lunch Lizbeth had retrieved from the milk separating room. Calving was messy, slippery work. Worse than cooking. Worse, even, than laundry.

John primed the water pump by lifting and lowering the long handle, and soon Lizbeth could tell by his rhythm that the tension in the handle had changed; water would sluice from the spout with the next pump.

As they had done when they were little, Lizbeth and John kicked off their shoes and socks and slapped their bare feet in the cold well water — "a pair of little ducks," their mother used to call them — as it spilled onto the smooth wooden platform. It was April, not yet warm enough for wet feet, and they laughed at the shock and daring. Lizbeth squealed when her brother flicked water at her with his fingers. Just as she was about to step away, he pumped the handle twice more, quickly, splashing her legs and soaking the hem of her dress. She hopped up and down in the puddle and vowed to get him back.

Shivering, they finally sat down on a dry corner of the wood to eat. The rubbery toes of chicken feet were like warm fingers against their cheeks as they chewed on the soles. John nudged Lizbeth with his elbow and laughed. "Hey, good job today," he said. "Too bad you can't cook as well as you can get dirty. Remember the last time you tried to make cracklings?"

"As if you'd ever let me forget," she said. Instead of rendering the fatty pork down to kernels of meat, she had started the contents of the pan on fire. There was still a singe mark on the wall behind the stove.

"And the cream gravy. I've seen fewer lumps in tapioca pudding."

"Haw haw. Very funny."

Later, when John went off to finish chores, Lizbeth returned to the house in an uncharacteristically helpful mood. There were bed sheets and the girls' slips to be washed. And her mother wanted to show her how to use the new-to-them wringer-washing machine, bought off the trading post.

"Heard you had yourself a little adventure," her mother said. She reached out and tucked a curl of hair behind Lizbeth's ear. "Now why don't we see whether you can master something you actually need to know. Be careful, the wringer will grab your arm as easily as it does a sleeve."

Once the linens had gone through the sloshing cycle, Lizbeth helped guide the heavy, sopping fabric through the rollers. Grey rinse water sluiced back into the basin to be used as wash water for the next load. As Lizbeth watched, her mind wandered and she forgot to be cautious, nearly getting her fingers caught. Her mother snatched them away and the sheet Lizbeth was about to guide through fell to the floor with a solid, wet thump.

Lizbeth was pretty certain her mother didn't know how to use a chair. Her skirt barely brushed the seat before she popped up like a piece of toast. Even when the entire family gathered around the table for breakfast, she always thought of "just one more thing" that needed doing. The brown sugar was missing from the table, or she had to to punch the bread dough down so it could rise again and be baked before lunch.

The other women from their village clucked with approval, maybe a little envy, and said things like, "Our Mrs. Klassen works like a whole dam full of beavers." Lizbeth thought they said dam with a little extra oomph. Probably because it wasn't possible for them to say the same syllable if it had a silent 'n' in it. Saying dam with an 'n' was tantamount to dropping a match in a pool of gasoline. You couldn't buy enough fire insurance for too many damns.

It was no wonder that her mother could never sit still. With Matthew still coming home to eat, she baked her way through a thousand pounds of flour a year, ground from their own grain. That was probably enough to feed one of the small mission countries they always got reports from in church. The reports came with a peg board of pictures, and Lizbeth remembered one photograph of a little black boy, looking pleased as peas, holding the severed heads of two grown men. One in each hand, by the hair. After that, Lizbeth figured the missionaries over there could probably use all the grain they could get, to keep the natives from getting hungry. She volunteered to send hers, because after the thousand pounds for the family, most of the rest of the harvest had to be sold to the farm co-op — where Mennonite wheat mixed with everyone else's, unlike themselves. Lizbeth's parents also set some aside to help poorer local families, or ones whose crops, for whatever reason, hadn't been good that year. They grew enough potatoes, too, that the kids joked about how they could end world hunger if they gave away the contents of their root cellar. Since the village was their whole world, Lizbeth didn't think it was that far from the truth.

"Come, Lizbeth. You can help me take these clothes back to the neighbours," her mother said. As one of their deliberate acts of kindness, they'd spent part of the afternoon washing and wringing the neighbours' clothes through their machine, and now the clean laundry needed to be returned next door and pinned on a sagging clothesline that spent more time as a perch for birds to shit from (it was okay to say shit but not damn, because anyone who kept cows knew that shit was just a fact of life).

Lizbeth couldn't stand their neighbours. The way they glanced over the fence as though any member of Lizbeth's family might, at any moment, attack them with the gospel, pelt them with Bible verses. When, in fact, all they ever did was give them potatoes and get their hands filthy trying to help them with their disgusting washing. Potatoes and laundry, it appeared, were as good a way as any to the soul.

Lizbeth didn't see the point. Not when the Heindricks were supposedly Mennonites, too, which meant they should be just as equipped to climb heaven's ladder as anyone else they knew. They should be able to fend for themselves. After all, it was their own fault they did things like keep guns and drink alcohol and that they never did anything kind for anyone. And as any Mennonite with half a wit knew, doing something bad at the same time as not doing something good meant you were moving in the wrong direction twice as fast.

"Don't we have enough of our own washing to do without having to muck around in theirs? Who knows where this has been," Lizbeth said, picking up a stiffened brown sock that they'd missed. She knew the neighbours' sons from school and, while she shared some of their finer views, that the village needed a movie theatre and a couple of stores, she wasn't impressed with them one bit. If anything, they hated the village in a way that made her want to defend everything about it.

The oldest of the Heindricks boys was named Luke and was John's age. Everyone at school called him Lucifer to keep from mixing him up with Lizbeth's third oldest brother. The other boy, Joel, was the same age as her. Both of the boys had dropped out after the sixth grade after Joel lost a hand in a freak threshing accident. Lizbeth thought it was just as well — not about the hand, of course. Just that more school for them would be like throwing pearls in the slop pail. Arithmetic wasn't going to make them become less creepy, either. They prowled around their family's five acres, shooting gophers in the face, laughing as though they'd done something clever.

Lizbeth rolled her eyes and called them *dummkopfs* behind their backs, but the truth was, she was afraid of them.

"I don't even want to know what kind of blood that was on their overalls," Lizbeth said, trying one last time to irritate her mother into letting her off the hook. "Probably all the gophers they ate for supper."

"Lizbeth, that's enough. I know it doesn't seem like it, but when we serve people with our hands, we serve them with our hearts. It can change them. And even if it doesn't — " She left the thought trailing and Lizbeth resisted the urge to tug and see if she could make it unravel.

She sighed as profoundly as she could, picked up a heavy basket of still-damp clothes and followed her mother out of their house and into the yard towards the neighbours.

"Been waitin' on these," Mrs. Heindricks said. She had come out of her house to meet them and closed the door behind her before Lizbeth or her mother could see inside. "Doesn't seem to me that your fancy machine takes any less time than a washboard and a determined pair of hands. And Lord knows you've got enough hands over there."

Lizbeth wondered how her mother managed to look so genuine. She was sure her own face had the word YUCK written all over it.

To Lizbeth's horror, her mother said, "Mr. Klassen asked me to say that he can use some extra help with the seeding this year, if your boys would like the work." Lizbeth pulled her head back, as though someone had grabbed her hair from behind. She screwed her eyebrows together, but her eyes widened in alarm when the two Heindricks boys suddenly came round the side of the house, startling her so that she nearly dropped her basket. One of them laughed, a cruel-sounding noise that came out his nose. He nudged his brother and said something Lizbeth couldn't quite hear — about working her over. She blushed down to her toes and felt she wanted to put on a fourth layer of clothes. Seeing the boys, Lizbeth's mother quickly stepped in front of her, and Lizbeth was surprised at how grateful, how safe she felt standing in that protective shadow.

"I wish we could just leave them be," Lizbeth said. It was a few days later and she and John had taken one of their mother's rhubarb-and-crabapple pies next door, and they had accepted it without so much as a mutter of thanks. "If you ask me, they wouldn't like it in heaven, anyway."

"It's not up to us. And God doesn't play favourites, Lizzy."

"He does so. He loved Jacob and hated Esau," she said with satisfaction.

"Well, still, it's not up to us to decide for someone else." He nudged Lizbeth off-balance and smiled, so quickly that it looked as though something else, shadowy, had moved across his features. "I think you should be careful, though." He was quiet for a moment, holding his thoughts. "Lizzy, listen to me, okay? God never said we have to trust our neighbours. Love is not the same thing as trust."

"Love is love and trust is trust. Got it," Lizbeth said, snickering. Although a stone had dropped into the pit of her stomach.

One day that summer, Lizbeth heard Lucifer and Joel talking over the fence to John, who was in the garden, weeding between the potato mounds.

"Hey, so your family's been so, um, kind and stuff, we decided we'd like to have a Bible study or something."

John stood up slowly and, after telling Lizbeth to stay put, walked towards them, but not all the way to the fence. Lizbeth pushed her fist into her stomach to stop it from flopping. Say no, she thought. But because they'd asked to hear about God, there was no way to refuse. After supper, John picked up his Bible, told their parents where he was going, and went out the door. When he came back an hour later, he looked bleached, as though someone had pulled a plug and let all his blood drain.

"What happened over there?" Lizbeth said. She took his Bible from him, set it on the kitchen table and pulled out a chair for him.

"I want you to promise me to stay as far away from them as you can," he said.

"Okay. But what happened? You're scaring me."

John didn't answer.

"I'm going to get Dad." Lizbeth turned to go, but John stopped her.

"Promise first," he said.

"I promise."

After they talked to John, their parents called together the whole family.

"From now on, none of you are to go near any one of those people by yourselves. And never into their house, under any circumstances. That includes your mother," Lizbeth's father said.

"What did they do?" Matthew said, always the most protective of the brothers. He leaned forward in his seat, searching John's face for an answer. John was looking down at his hands. His whole body was shaking.

"This is not to go farther than this house," Lizbeth's father said. He told them how when John went to the neighbours', the Heindricks boys had set up a game for him. "Bible roulette," they called it. One of them produced a hunting rifle and aimed it at John.

"I wouldn't get any answers wrong if I were you," the one with the rifle had said. And when John stumbled over the begats, he shot a hole in their own house, right next to John's head.

"Can't you call the police?" Lizbeth said. "They can take them to jail and we'll never have to worry."

"We called," her mother said, her voice unsteady.

"And?"

"The boy's parents convinced them it was an accident. They took them to town, anyway, but will probably be released before long."

"Shouldn't we tell the rest of the village?" Matthew said.

"Right. And the pastor and elders. Have them driven out!" Lizbeth said.

"For now, no," their father said. "The boys threatened John not to tell anyone. I think the best thing is to pray, ask God to change their hearts."

John began to lose weight after his ordeal next door. His confident, teasing way also changed, became an effort, something Lizbeth thought he only did to keep her from noticing the dark smudges under his eyes.

Over the next several weeks, because nothing else happened, just the occasional leering gesture over the fence, things gradually slipped back into a tense version of normal. In the fall, during the days, Lucifer and Joel disappeared into the far corner of their family's acres to shoot, or were heard gunning their rusty old truck down the gravel road towards town. They'd come back, a day or two later, and Lizbeth would hear their rough laughter through the open window of her mother's kitchen.

But when their truck broke down at the beginning of winter, the tension between John and the two boys worsened. Sometimes she heard them shout taunts as John pulled up the tractor to plough snow from the driveway. Their voices were harsh, like the sound of heavy canvas being torn.

"Hey, Bible Boy!" they'd say. Once, from the kitchen window, Lizbeth saw them point their shotgun at him, Joel propping the barrel on the stump of his wrist. "Why don't you come on over here and see if you can save us."

Lizbeth had flown out of the house into the cold, but it was already over and John walked back with her, making her promise again to stay away from them.

That night, Lizbeth sunk down on her knees in front of her bed. She fumbled with the soft rag rug she always kept by her feet, pushing it to the side until she knelt directly on the wood floor. On either side of her, her sisters were already asleep and snoring. Lizbeth began to pray.

She prayed again the next night, and the next. All winter.

By spring though, Lizbeth was distracted from her prayers when Liam Rempel, who was in her grade, started stealing looks at her in class when his teacher-father wasn't looking. And on the morning that everything changed forever, there was no prickle at the back of her neck to make her think anything might be particularly wrong. No flutter of angel's wings in the corner of Lizbeth's vision, which her Sunday school teacher once said had warned him away from a mad dog. She hadn't noticed any tension in the air. Rather, white Saskatoon-berry flowers had bloomed overnight and made the landscape look covered up with cleanliness.

"Hey, Lizzy," John said when Lizbeth left the house that morning, carrying several of her mother's fresh *rollkuchen* wrapped in a tea towel. She'd snuck them when her mother wasn't looking, and they were still warm and smelled pleasantly greasy. "Those for me?"

"Um, no," she said, teasing. "You can have all the ones I made. Better be quick though, before Mom gives them to the pigs."

Lizbeth kept walking and willed John not to follow her or ask any more questions. The *rollkuchen* were for Liam. And for once, Lizbeth had stopped wondering what else there was in the world. *Rollkuchen* and a Rempel was about as Mennonite as things could get, but Liam had a knack for getting into and out of mild trouble. Like the time he left a firecracker on the wood-heating stove at school, and when it went off, stood up and soon had the class laughing with a short lesson on pacifism. Imagining a life with him made Lizbeth think that life in the village might have some potential, after all.

Lizbeth met Liam at the disused railroad tracks that ran behind an overgrown row of wild chokecherries at the back of their property. The same bushes that Lizbeth, with her mother and sisters, picked from every September for syrup and jelly.

Lizbeth and Liam walked together, at first only holding hands. It was enough to make Lizbeth feel as though her heart, which was thumping like a twitterpated rabbit, would suddenly stutter to a stop from happiness. And she was sure she'd die from guilt and joy when, Liam, humming a melody, swept her around and began to show her how to waltz.

"Hey, you're pretty good," Liam said. "You do know this is the Devil's footwork, don't you?"

Lizbeth's ears became hot. "Yeah, well."

"You know why Mennonites don't dance, don't you?"

"Uh-uh," Lizbeth said, mentally kicking herself for having nothing clever to say.

"I heard my mom whispering it to a bunch of ladies once."

"Yeah, okay. So tell me already."

"Mennonites don't dance because it might lead to sex." He twirled her around and when she spun to face him, she saw that his face was as red as hers. "I can't believe I said that." He stopped and stared down at his feet. "Sorry."

"Um. It's okay." Lizbeth pushed her toes through the dirt. Secretly, she was already planning to re-live the moment in her imagination, turning it over and over and savouring it like a lozenge. So when the first shot rang out, Lizbeth stupidly thought it meant they'd been caught.

"Probably just a fox near the henhouse." Liam said. When they heard the second shot, followed by a woman's scream, Lizbeth's heart became a plug in her chest. Liam grabbed her hand and pulled her towards her house. She stumbled, and couldn't move except to clutch her arms and bend forward. Her hair, which she had let down so Liam could see it looking soft and loose, fell in front of her shoulders and hid her face.

"No-no-no-no-no." The moan seeped from her like air from a tire.

"Lizzy," Liam said. But hearing John's pet name for her in Liam's mouth only made her feel the need to retch. No one else called her Lizzy.

"Lizzy. C'mon. We have to go." When Lizbeth tried to run, she couldn't make her legs obey. They felt like dough and moved in all the wrong ways.

Liam stopped to look into Lizbeth's face before he turned and ran towards the sound of the shot. Alone on the crumbling tracks, Lizbeth watched him disappear.

Afterwards, Lizbeth would not remember how she got back to the house but, when she caught up with Liam, he was kneeling in her parent's garden, cradling John's body. The front of Liam's shirt was soaked through and sticking to his chest with her brother's blood, which had stopped pouring from a hole in his neck. Her mother had run back to the house to call for help that was already too late.

"He asked for you," Liam said, his head bowed. "When I got here, he said your name."

Lizbeth stood, stiff and still, her legs rooted to where she had stopped. Her mother and sisters came running from the house, and she watched them as though they weren't real. Her father and brothers, who heard the shot from a nearby field they'd been working, came next. One by one, they knelt around John, reaching out for his and each other's hands, and wept. Their father, his voice breaking on every word, began to pray. For strength to bear this loss, and for the souls of the boys who had killed their son and brother. Lizbeth didn't kneel with them and didn't bow her head. She continued to stand and kept her eyes open and fixed on John.

When a police officer finally came from the city, he said, "I doubt those boys'll be back, but let us know if you see them and we'll bring them in." He folded his notebook. "We'll do what we can."

The officer was right. The Heindricks boys never did return.

Except for the first days that followed her brother's death, the whole year that Lizbeth was fourteen was a dark blur, like looking from a window of a train at night. All the pages of the calendar had been compressed to fit into a few small squares labelled Visit from Pastor Enns 8 PM. Viewing at church 7:30. Funeral 12 noon.

When it was over, Lizbeth couldn't recall her brother's funeral the way she knew it must have happened. In the few pictures, it was a clear spring day and someone had cut the grass around the church. The smell of green would have bled freshness from the tip of each broken blade. What she saw when she closed her eyes though, was not a clear bright sky, but a heavy grey wrapping of clouds.

Inside, on the men's side of the church Lizbeth's father and brothers sat, sorrow and acceptance scrawled in a collective expression. Across the aisle, Lizbeth was surrounded by her mother and sisters, as well as aunts and the women who made it their business, Sunday or not, to attend everything going on inside God's house.

When her father and brothers carried John's coffin outside to the cemetery that lay next to the church like a garden of stone, Lizbeth felt utterly alone. As John was lowered into the hole dug for him, Lizbeth clutched a bouquet of flowers that she was supposed to throw, along with her grief, into the grave before dirt was shovelled over the top. It was as though they were planting him in the ground so he'd be ready for the heavenly harvest to come.

They buried John without Lizbeth's flowers, which were left where she stood, all torn petals and bruised stems. The mourners from the community, followed by Lizbeth's family, gradually left the gravesite. Lizbeth was the last to walk away.

At home, Lizbeth's mother and sisters quietly set out a light lunch for family that came from other villages and the Hutterite colony. As younger cousins played, looking nervously at one another, unsure of what was all right to say, Lizbeth's aunts made their rounds, offering powdery-smelling embraces along with looks of sympathy that felt, to Lizbeth, as empty as wheat husks. Uncles sat in the living room cracking whole nuts, talking intermittently about the weather and God's unknowable ways.

While everyone was busy, or simply not paying attention, Lizbeth saw her parents leave the house with a plate of food. She followed, hiding behind the skirt of a tree, as they walked up to the Heindricks' house and knocked on the door.

At first, she couldn't hear what they were saying, until Mr. and Mrs. Heindricks' voices began to rise.

"Don't need any of your pity here," Mrs. Heindricks said, her voice pelting Lizbeth's parents like sharp stones.

"In different ways, we've both lost sons," Lizbeth's father said. "The Lord calls his people to be compassionate and mourn with those who mourn. And to forgive."

"Don't need your forgiveness, either. If you want us to go, we told you our price," Mr. Heindricks said and knocked twice on the siding of his house. The words hit her father as though he'd been spat on. Lizbeth waited for him, for her mother, to turn their backs and leave. To stay and shout. Just to do anything. But they lowered their voices until Lizbeth could no longer hear. Moments later, her father reached out and shook the other man's hand.

When they finally walked away, Lizbeth stepped out to meet them.

"How could you talk to them after they — " Lizbeth said, her voice brittle. "They aren't even sorry."

"Lizbeth," her father said.

"When someone murders your son, you don't pray for them. And you don't take them a plate of food or buy their house."

"Lizbeth, they didn't take John's life. Their boys did."

"Yeah, well. They didn't stop them, either," Lizbeth said, her voice strengthening on a gust of anger. Before her parents could reply, she turned and walked away. As she did, she heard her father tell her mother to let her go, that she needed time. Lizbeth knew that there wasn't enough time on God's entire calendar for whatever it was they thought she needed. So she planted her grief like a seedling in the ground and watered it with anger. At times, she even spoke to it to help it grow.

Within a month, as Lizbeth watched from the kitchen window, her parents helped the Heindricks' move out of the house next door. Before they drove away, her father handed them a thick envelope containing payment for their property. Enough for them to start a different life somewhere else where no one knew them. And once they were gone, Lizbeth's family would never again have to have such close neighbours.

Afterwards, Lizbeth's mother came inside and found her at the window. She stroked her hair gently. "Maybe you can help me with some cleaning next door. Your brothers are going to take down that fence later. We'll have the house for storage and both gardens to plant next year."

"You can't make me go over there." Lizbeth turned and looked at her mother to make sure she understood. "Not ever."

A few weeks later, Lizbeth overheard one of her aunts talking to her mother. "When she's a few years older and marries herself a good husband, has a house of her own to take care of, that'll be what helps her. One of the Rempel boys, maybe. In church, before all this business with the neighbours, I thought I saw the youngest one looking her way."

"I really don't know," Lizbeth's mother said. "Maybe."

Lizbeth could no longer think of Liam without seeing him soaked in her brother's blood. She stopped speaking to him at school, and when they both started taking the bus to the high school in town, she spent the ride with her face hidden behind a textbook, studying. She found that if she kept her mind busy it was almost enough to keep her from thinking about what had happened. As long as she was working out math and science and history problems, she wouldn't pull at the threads that dangled in her thoughts. If she hadn't met with Liam that day, if she hadn't walked off with her stolen *rollkuchen*, cancelling her prayers with sin, he would still be alive. Now there was no going back.

When Lizbeth was seventeen, after she'd been a bridesmaid in Matthew, Mary and Ruth's weddings, she graduated from high school and took a filing job at the agriculture research station near the edge of town. Her father drove her in the mornings and picked her up after work, but when Lizbeth received her first paycheque, she found she had enough money left after taxes to rent a basement apartment. She'd be able to walk to work and back.

The apartment had one bedroom that was only inches bigger than the twin bed she took with her from her parents' house. There was a sitting area outside the bedroom. And, in a corner next to the bathroom, a tiny kitchen, with a tiny countertop fridge and an enormous brown microwave arranged on a table against the back wall, next to a sink.

Lizbeth's mother unpacked a box filled with a few plates and some cutlery. There was a medium-sized pot and a percolator, but Lizbeth had refused a mixing bowl and rolling pin. "How will you keep busy? There's nothing to cook with."

"It'll be fine," Lizbeth said, impatient for her mother to leave. "I'll get lots of rest after work. And there's a cafeteria there. I can buy a punch card."

"Cafeteria food is not food," her mother said and went to have a talk with the people who lived upstairs and owned the house.

"How would you know?" Lizbeth said after she was gone. She looked around at the few pieces of furniture that were now hers. Matthew had bought a large orange-and-brown chesterfield that morning from the trading post and donated it to the cause of giving Lizbeth something to sit on. All day her family had come and gone, bringing things and remarking on the impossibly small size of the space. It's smaller than the summer kitchen! There isn't enough room in that little fridge for a pail of eggs!

After everyone else drifted back to the farm, Lizbeth sat down on her couch as though she'd never before in her life had the time. She tried to do nothing but bask in the empty hours until it was late enough to go to bed.

Soon she started to pick at balls of lint on the seat cushions until she had a fuzzy pile. She got up to drop them in the garbage and decided to measure the dimensions of her new home by counting how many steps it took to get from one end to the other, the same way her father used to guesstimate the length of things.

There were eighteen steps in one direction if she walked from the front wall straight into the tin shower that dripped one drop of water every three seconds. Twenty-one steps in the other direction, over top of the chesterfield to the door that led outside, to the cement doorwell that would collect dust and wind-blown newspapers if not faithfully swept. Approximately three hundred and seventy-eight square feet, less or more.

Although there were four sets of curtains hung in the apartment, there were only two windows — the one in the bedroom was so small and high that Lizbeth had to stand on her bed to peer out. There were four patterns of embossed wallpaper, two clashing colours of wall-to-wall carpeting that were laid with opposing naps. And a potted plant that was a housewarming gift from her sister-in-law, but wouldn't survive the week without natural light.

Lizbeth's landlords were an old Mennonite couple, which was the only way her parents had finally consented to the move. It seemed to help ease their concerns that the Giesbrechts, when they met them, smelled of liniment and had, against Lizbeth's repeated objections, promised her parents they'd look after her like their own daughter.

"I'm trying to not feel like someone's daughter for once," Lizbeth had said to her mother.

"Well, I'm sorry to hear that," her mother said. "But you are my daughter and you can't get away from that, no matter how far you go."

"That's not what I meant. And this is hardly far." Lizbeth flung her arm in the general direction of home. "Fifteen minutes. Less if Dad or Matthew drives like they're late for supper."

Already, old Mrs. Giesbrecht had kept her word with an enormous crockery dish filled with farmer's sausage and both Saskatoon berry and cottage cheese *varenyky*, covered in heavy cream gravy.

When she had brought it down, Lizbeth had thanked her, but after closing the door, she rolled her eyes and muttered to herself, "No wonder we're all as fat as cheese." She intended to make toast for supper and, in a few days, buy a salad cookbook. And then, who knew? Maybe she'd even buy a pair of slacks, if she could find a flattering pair.

As Lizbeth ran out of things in the apartment to count, she opened the fridge and reasoned that one more day of cream gravy wouldn't make any difference. She took out the casserole dish, leaned against the table and began to fork up mouthfuls of cold *varenyky*, the congealed gravy coating her tongue with memories of home.

Lizbeth thought about her mother and felt a twinge of longing that she quickly swallowed down. But it kept rising to the surface and soon she thought of the smell of bread baking in the morning, her sisters in the kitchen, of John and his appetite, the way he used to eat a whole loaf, all by himself, every day. What had happened to all that extra bread? After John died, did their mother make less dough every day? Or did everyone take their share of what he'd left behind? An extra hundred pounds of flour a year. It had to go somewhere.

Lizbeth put her fork down, lowered her forehead slowly into her hands and sank into the one kitchen chair that she'd been able to fit into the apartment. Loneliness washed over her until she felt she would drown.

That night she lay in bed, tears wetting her hair, and wondered whether she'd ever stop being her dead brother's sister.

On Sundays, Lizbeth went to church in town. Afterwards, she walked back to her apartment and waited for Matthew to pick her up and drive her to the farm for lunch. After a few months she began to make excuses. She didn't tell her family that she'd met a young man, a lab assistant, at work, and on Sundays he picked her up outside the church, with a picnic of Chinese food in the back seat of his car, and took her for long drives in the country.

She felt sorry for lying to them, but when Lizbeth was with Ben she was able to pack everything he didn't know about her into a box in her mind and set it aside. It was only later, when he dropped her off at home, that her thoughts wouldn't stay tucked away.

On one Sunday drive, when they had parked to watch a storm approach on the horizon, Lizbeth slipped and told Ben that she'd like him to meet her family someday. Ben, in her imagination, stood between her and her family, both a fence and a bridge.

He was quiet for what seemed like a long time.

"I don't think I want to," he said.

"Oh — "

"Wait," he said, reaching across the seat and pressing a finger to her mouth. "The thing is, it only matters who you are to me. This person, right here, right now." He placed two fingers lightly on her chest, above her heart. "Don't you see? Meeting someone's family always messes that up. I'd end up seeing you differently, through their eyes. And I don't want that."

Lizbeth looked down at her hands. She wasn't sure what Ben meant. He had a way of making things sound too profound to argue with. The things her family talked about had always been so black and white, like the onionskin pages of her father's Bible. Ever since the first time Ben talked to her on their lunch hour, it was as though everything she'd ever thought began to turn into shades of grey. They had long discussions about things like pollution, and the Prime Minister's ignorance of the western provinces. But he was also sweet, and left notes, along with cold Jamaican beef patties wrapped in plastic, in the pocket of her sweater at work. Sometimes, he parked outside her apartment at night until she turned out her light. When she noticed him there she flicked her lights on and off and he answered with his headlights before driving away. It became their routine. And eventually, when Lizbeth went to bed at night, she was sometimes able to sleep without thinking of home.

"Hey, so, I think your landlady saw me parked outside your house last night," Ben said one morning at work. He rolled his eyes and snorted softly, the same way he did when he talked about his supervisor, a middle-aged man whose unconvincing comb-over and big ears, watery eyes and drooping eyelids, made him look slow witted. Lizbeth didn't think he was slow but kept the thought to herself.

"How do you know?" Lizbeth said, nearly dropping the files she was carrying. Suddenly she imagined what Mrs. Giesbrecht might think of her, a young woman who was followed home by a strange man. And although she tried to pretend that it didn't matter, Lizbeth worried that Mrs. Giesbrecht might have already called her parents.

"The ol' girl came out with her bloomers in a bunch and told me 'Nice young men don't park outside a young lady's home.'" Ben imitated Mrs. Giesbrecht's voice, high and scolding, making Lizbeth laugh a little.

"What did you say to her?"

Without looking to see whether they were alone, Ben reached out, tucked a stray twist of hair behind Lizbeth's ear and softly kissed her cheek. "I told her I was just looking out for you."

Lizbeth leaned towards his voice, letting herself fall into it.

The following Sunday, when Ben pulled up in front of the church, Lizbeth got into his car and didn't say anything until he asked what was wrong.

For several minutes she didn't tell him that her parents had called her the night before, asking questions about the young man in the car.

"He's a friend from work," she'd said to her mother, and again when her father got on the phone.

"What kind of friend is he? Do you know his parents? Are they Mennonite? Do they even go to church?"

"He's a good friend. And no, I don't know his parents. He isn't Mennonite. And he doesn't go to church, but he doesn't mind if I do."

"Doesn't mind." Her father's voice cinched tight and Lizbeth could almost see the worried expression on his face. "What, exactly, is that supposed to mean?"

"It means that maybe he will some day. Who knows? Aren't we supposed to witness to unbelievers so they can become believers?"

After arguing, nothing was resolved except Lizbeth had promised she'd bring Ben out to meet them.

Now, in the car she said, "It's my family. They know about us." Her stomach knotted. "It's been weeks since I've been home. It's just that they're worried about me. They don't know you."

"Well, it's hardly a secret," he said, as though it was a little absurd that she hadn't told them before. "But I guess we'd better go out there and put them at ease." He was smiling, but Lizbeth could see that the corners of his mouth were tense.

"Really? You'd do that? I know how you feel about — "

Ben stopped her. "For you, anything," he said, turning serious. He shifted the car into gear and they drove to her parents' village in silence.

All through lunch Lizbeth was uncomfortably aware of everyone around the table, including Ben. Luke still lived at home and Matthew and his wife were there, too. She had never thought about it before, but next to her Sunday-groomed brothers, Ben looked sloppily put together in faded jeans and longish hair. He didn't know not to talk about politics on Sunday, and was deliberately vague when asked personal questions about himself and how he and Lizbeth knew each other.

And then there was the food — *pluma moos* and *zwieback*, cold meats and potatoes fried in lard — which seemed so simple and farmsy next to the exotic things Ben had taught her to like. She offered a silent prayer of thanks that there were no chicken feet to go with the chicken soup, and that John wasn't there to tease her with them.

"Lizzy, here, is a great girl, Mr. Klassen." Ben spoke between polite bites of sausage. Lizbeth wished everyone would just stop talking. "She may not have told you, but she's indispensable around the office."

"I see," Lizbeth's father said. He folded his hands, leaned back in his chair and looked at Ben as though he was an over-assertive rooster that might be ready for the soup pot. Chop-chop, nothing personal.

When Lizbeth reached for a bun, Ben stopped her by gently catching her hand. "I thought you were trying to cut back."

"Right. No, you're right," she said. She glanced at her father before she turned her attention to sweeping a spray of crumbs from the table into her hand and brushing them into her plate.

After lunch, Lizbeth followed her mother into the kitchen to help wash up, leaving Ben to drink coffee with her father and brothers. Lizbeth wished for her sisters, who usually helped blitz through the dishes in a matter of minutes and could talk steadily about village gossip the whole time.

"Lizbeth, you don't even know his family," her mother said after a while. Lizbeth could tell she was being deliberately slow with the dishcloth. "He doesn't seem right for you."

"What's that supposed to mean?" Lizbeth said. She scrunched a tea towel into a glass tumbler and gave it an anxious twist.

"He makes me nervous, the way he doesn't want to talk about the two of you. And he seems very overprotective. You need someone who will be sensitive, who will understand where you come from."

"Are you trying to say I'm supposed to find someone simple?" Lizbeth said, teetering on the edge of angrier words. "If he's overprotective, at least that makes one person around here who's willing to look after the people they care about."

"Lizbeth. We're your family. We've always looked out for you."

"Sure. Like you looked out for John? If I was murdered in the garden, you'd all just forgive the person who did it and go on with your lives and eat more bread." Lizbeth looked at her mother, who seemed confused, and had taken a step back as though pushed. Another step and she'd lose her balance. "If something happened to me and Ben didn't do something about it, he'd never, ever get over it. He'd be miserable the rest of his life."

"Oh, Lizbeth. Is that's how you think we should be, too?" her mother said. "I'm so sorry you feel that way. But you know we loved your brother as much as you did. We grieved for him as much as you."

"No, I don't know that." Lizbeth was breathing hard and stumbling over her thoughts.

Later, in Ben's car as he drove them back to town, Lizbeth stared out the passenger window as the countryside slipped by.

"Your father told me what happened," Ben said. Lizbeth knew that he meant what had happened to John.

"Do you see me differently now?" she said without turning to look at him.

"No," he said. "You're you. That hasn't changed."

But when Lizbeth tried to focus on her reflection in the glass, it shifted and blurred with the changing horizon.

On a Wednesday afternoon, three months after they'd met, and without telling anyone, Lizbeth and Ben went to City Hall.

Lizbeth wore a white dress she bought off the rack at Woolworth. She repeated her vows with grave attention and listened as the judge called her by her new name. She was Mrs. Ben Bryant. A name she'd never heard in her whole life until she met him.

"Mrs. Bryant," she said, trying to pull it over her head like a new dress. But it was more like an apron that left her old clothes showing.

Afterwards, when they left the building, she sat on the front steps and cried.

"I don't understand you, Lizzy," Ben said, a little roughly. There were people coming up and down the stairs and all of them were either looking at her or trying not to.

"It's just — "

"Is it because your folks weren't here?" He crouched down beside her so he could tip up her chin and look into her eyes. "Lizzy, I thought we were going to be enough for each other. That we didn't need anyone else."

She was quiet for a few moments longer. "No, you're right," she said and let him help her up. She took a deep breath and held onto it for as long as she could.

When Ben was offered a research position in Calgary that meant they'd be able to afford a house and Lizbeth would no longer have to work, they packed up the few things they owned and moved.

At first, Ben took Lizbeth to places like the zoo and rode with her on the newly built C-Train so they could see the city together. They went to an Indian restaurant, Taj, sandwiched between a linens store and a bookshop in Kensington. They bought a few pieces of new furniture together and Lizbeth busied herself decorating their house in the north end.

For weeks, Lizbeth spent her mornings at home looking through the Yellow Pages, which sat comfortably on her lap like a soft, flexible weight, and tore out pages with places they could visit on weekends. Museums, heritage sites, bird sanctuaries, long walks along the Bow River that took them downtown where the tall buildings seemed to close snugly around them like fingers.

In the afternoons, when she was alone, she explored the nearby Nose Hill Park where, in the distance, if she climbed to the top of the long, meandering path, she could see a blue ridge of mountains. She picked wild flowers and carried them home to arrange in jam jars, which she set out around the house.

After work, in the evenings, Ben sometimes brought home spicy curries with mango pickle, dhal, and chapattis. The exotic spices made Lizbeth feel as though she could step outside herself and into a different skin, as though who she was really was only a garment. She could decide to be different if she wanted to.

When the newness of the city faded and was no longer a distraction, homesickness began to pull at her. Without meaning to, she thought of cooking with her mother and sisters in their old kitchen, her brothers coming in for lunch. She thought of John, the games they used to play, his blood on Liam's shirt. She saw the hole in his neck and his casket being lowered into the ground. Her parents knelt and wept by his body, betraying him with their forgiveness. And she could have stopped all of it from happening if she hadn't chosen to meet Liam that day.

"Why do you think about all that stuff? You're making yourself sick," Ben said. He didn't hide his disgust when he woke up one morning to find Lizbeth throwing up in the bathroom. "Why don't you go do something? Keep busy."

"Maybe I'm sick of you. Did you ever think about that?" Lizbeth reached over and shoved the door closed. Later she came out and apologized.

"I don't feel very well lately," she said.

The more Lizbeth slipped into herself, the more Ben became brooding and distant. Whenever he thought Lizbeth was in a sulk, he left her at home and went for long drives by himself. Sometimes he came back with a gift-shop trinket from Banff, or a new kind of food, Thai or sushi. But when they didn't cheer her up, Lizbeth could tell that he was giving up on her.

"It's just self-indulgence," Ben said. "All this feeling sorry for yourself. That's all it is. You're being selfish. I didn't think you were like this." He had come home late one evening to find her sitting in the dark. It was a Sunday and he'd been gone since morning.

"Like what?"

"Like someone who can't make up her own mind to be happy without a bunch of external stuff."

Lizbeth laughed flatly.

"That's funny," she said. "And here I've spent the entire day trying to figure out how to tell you that I'm pregnant." She threw the words at him and wondered whether he'd think it too external of her if she decided to be happy about the baby.

Lizbeth gave birth to their daughter, Magda, on a freezing winter morning. The kind of morning that was thrillingly cold and, when she was younger, had made her feel as though the air would freeze in her lungs if she inhaled too deeply.

In the car, on the way to the hospital, Lizbeth panted through the pain in her belly and back and legs, her breath coating the windshield with a fine sheet of ice that Ben had to scrape away with his driver's license in order to see. He was quiet all the way there, and all through the delivery while Lizbeth let the waves of agony push everything else around her out of focus. The pain was like dark water, pulling her under, until the nurse put Magda in Lizbeth's arms for the first time. At that moment, the water suddenly drained away, leaving her cold.

Lizbeth looked at her daughter's downy head. She drew her finger over her soft, pink forehead and cheeks, over her nose and mouth. She uncurled her long fingers and counted them.

"She looks like my mother," Lizbeth said. She closed her eyes and leaned back into her pillow, shuddering with a wave of homesickness. When she opened her eyes, she expected Ben to say something, be annoyed that she'd seen anything in their daughter but the two of them. But Ben surprised her by taking out a new camera he'd bought and snapping a picture.

"My two girls," he said and kissed Lizbeth on her forehead. The warmth of his mouth spread over her and felt something like joy.

For a moment, Lizbeth believed they'd go home and Magda would fill the space between them. They'd be a family.

Lizbeth doted nervously over Magda, worried at each sound she made, each sound she didn't.

At first, she kept up almost feverishly with the housekeeping, cooking simple dishes from a cookbook for beginners. Creamed peas on toast. Hamburger and mushroom soup casserole.

Soon, though, pockets of laundry began to accumulate around the house, which Lizbeth pushed together with the side of her foot to form fewer, larger piles that she sent tumbling down the stairs into the basement where she could almost forget about them. In the kitchen, dishes filled the sink and cans of food sat, half-eaten, flaked tuna turned fishy and green.

Lizbeth tried to sleep when Magda did, but worry kept her awake even in the afternoon. She imagined waking to find Magda had disappeared into thin air, as though she'd never existed. Except that Lizbeth would know what was missing by the piece of herself that was also gone.

Once, when Magda suddenly stopped crying and Lizbeth thought she wasn't breathing, she pinched her hard, making her screech and leaving a mark on her leg.

"What the hell did you think you were doing?" Ben said when he saw the red welt.

"I just thought — " Lizbeth said, fighting herself to keep from crying useless tears. "I don't know. My mother always knew what to do."

"Of course she did. She had a hundred children," Ben said.

"When my youngest brother used to fuss, I remember her giving him a dropper of something," Lizbeth said, a gurgle of hope rising into her voice. She laughed a little. "But I don't know what it was."

"Yeah, well that doesn't surprise me much. It's no wonder you make yourself miserable, what with no one holding a dropper over you all the time. I suppose you wish she was here to do everything for you now."

"No. I don't. Really."

"We're your family," he said. "Me and Magda. I don't know why that can't be enough for you." He left the house, slamming the door behind him.

When he was gone, Lizbeth whispered to herself, "It is enough, it is. It is."

The next day, when Ben hadn't returned, Lizbeth stood in her kitchen, swinging Magda in her arms in a wide arc to stop her from crying.

"Please stop, baby. Please stop crying for Mommy. I don't know what to do for you," she said, the words crumbling out of her mouth like dry toast. The more Lizbeth tried, the more Magda refused to be comforted. Finally Lizbeth strapped Magda into her baby seat and placed her on the kitchen table. She sat on a chair across from her, pulled her bare feet up onto the seat and, as Magda wailed, lowered her face to her knees. Her heart pounded so heavily in her chest that it felt like a ball being bounced against a wall. Finally, she couldn't stand it any longer, and had to get up.

She walked back and forth across the kitchen, opening cupboards, noisily pulling out pots and bowls and an old wooden rolling pin. She swept a hedge of dirty dishes into the sink and took out a bag of flour, scooping some into a metal bowl. She broke eggs against the side of the bowl, letting bits of shell slip in. She added a spoonful of salt and dribbles of water and mixed until the dough seemed like it might be right. She turned it out onto the counter and gathered it into a ball, pressing it with her knuckles over and over, kneading and kneading, desperate to make the dough feel the same as her mother's.

When she rolled the dough out and cut it into pockets to fill with cottage cheese, the seams kept coming apart. She wet them with water and tried to press them back together, but the dough became thin and gluey at the edges and, when she dropped them into boiling water, the *varenyky* opened and escaped curds churned in the pot until all there was to scoop onto a plate were soggy flags of empty dough and rubbery, boiled cheese. Trembling, and with the sound of Magda still crying behind her, Lizbeth covered the dough with lumps of floury cream gravy and ate bent over the countertop until she felt sick and empty at the same time. She crammed the dirty pots into the sink, picked up Magda and carried her to bed, ignoring the smell of her soiled diaper. Lizbeth lay down with Magda stinking and crying beside her. In the middle of the night, when it was darkest, Lizbeth picked up the phone.

"I don't need — " Lizbeth said when she heard her mother's voice. "I just — " Her mother said something Lizbeth couldn't remember later. After a little while she fumbled the phone back onto its cradle and fell asleep.

Lizbeth woke the next day, not knowing what time it was. Someone had opened her curtains and she could tell that the sun was already above the house. She reached beside her, pressed her hand into the spot where Magda had been and was dimly aware that a good mother should be worried. But instead of getting up she turned onto her back and tented her knees. She rubbed her face and stared at the ceiling until, from the kitchen, Lizbeth heard the sound of Magda laughing.

Magda doesn't laugh, Lizbeth thought.

Still in the same clothes from the day before, Lizbeth got up slowly and walked down the hallway, thinking Ben must have come home, even though the house smelled clean and he never helped with the housework. Or with Magda.

The house was tidy. The washer and dryer hummed in the basement and the windows had all been opened to let in fresh air. The smell of bleach wafted crisply from the bathroom and, in the kitchen, where Lizbeth found her mother bouncing Magda on her hip, clean dishes were stacked, drip-drying in a rack next to the sink, ready to be wiped and put away.

Relief flooded over Lizbeth as she stood just outside the kitchen watching as her mother moved easily from the sink to the stove, where there was a pot on the boil, its lid rattling with the steam of chokecherries being made into syrup. Her mother's shoulders were round and relaxed, as though she was as familiar with Lizbeth's kitchen as her own, as though they'd never had to carry any weight for very long.

"Mom, I didn't expect you to come," Lizbeth said. Her voice was dry and cracked when she spoke, and she stiffened a little when her mother turned towards her. "When I called last night. It was late. I didn't mean for you to — " She stopped and thought. "How did you get here?"

"Wouldn't you know it, there's a bus that comes right from Swift Current to Calgary," her mother said. "I could hardly believe how easy it was. All I had to do was sit and listen for the driver to tell me we were here. And there were taxis right there outside the front doors of the depot. I gave them your address and, next thing I knew, I was here. You should keep your door locked in the city."

Lizbeth looked around and noticed a large suitcase balanced on the seats of two chairs in front of the table. She had never known her parents to own a suitcase, but there it was, flung open to reveal a nest of different-sized bowls, a flour sifter and a bundle of wooden spoons and other tools. Taking up one whole side was an open Styrofoam box containing a raw chicken and an ice cream pail of frozen Saskatoon berries.

"I brought a few things. I didn't know what you'd have," Lizbeth's mother said.

"Mom, I'm fine. Really. I said I didn't need anything." Lizbeth became silent.

"I've already made the noodles for the soup and the chicken is ready to go in the pot," her mother said.

The chicken, with its neck tucked into its breast and feet still attached, was still dimpled from when its feathers had been plucked, probably a day or two ago. It was so fresh it looked as though it had had a sudden chill.

"I can't believe you brought a chicken on the bus, Mom. We have chickens here, you know."

"Yes, but this one's from home." Lizbeth's mother came up to her and lifted Magda off her own hip and into Lizbeth's arms.

"She's beautiful."

"She looks like you, Mom. Every time I look at her, I see you."

"I noticed that. Cries like you used to, though." She was quiet for a moment as she unscrewed the cap of Lizbeth's salt shaker and poured some into the chicken pot. "I'll tell you a secret if you like. A dropper of brandy does the same trick for her as it did with all my babies."

"Brandy," Lizbeth said. "You can't be serious."

"Your dad always had to go to the French village down the road to get it. It was the only thing that calmed you down enough to see that things weren't as bad as they seemed."

"Maybe that's my problem. I should drink."

"Well, nobody ever said it was a long-term solution. At some point, there has to be something else. Now, why don't you go have a bath? My granddaughter and I will take care of things in here," she said, taking Magda back.

When Lizbeth returned to the kitchen after a long shower that left her skin hot and tingling, she found Magda asleep in her baby seat on the table. The chicken was floating in a pot on the stove, along with slices of onions, chopped carrots and whole anise seeds. Lazy bubbles rose up to the surface from the bottom of the pot.

Lizbeth picked up one of her mother's spoons and tried to push the chicken's scaly yellow feet under the water. They bobbed back up, refusing to stay down. Even when she pressed the lid down on top, they toed their way out.

"You and John always fought over those silly feet," Lizbeth's mother said. She pulled a large metal bowl from her suitcase, set it on the counter and broke eggs, one in each hand, against the side. The sound to Lizbeth, as the eggs rang against the bowl, was like a call to worship. Lizbeth watched as her mother poured in cream and blended it together with the flour until the dough started to come into a ball.

"*Rollkuchen*," her mother said simply when Lizbeth peered into the bowl. "It was always your favourite, wasn't it."

"You always made everything look so easy. I've never been able to figure out how you do that."

"You just let go and let it happen." Her mother scraped the contents of the bowl onto the counter and dusted it with a puff of flour. She took Lizbeth's hands in hers and showed her how to knead the dough until it was soft and elastic — by pushing it away from her with the heels of her hands, turning it a quarter turn, and pulling it back towards her with her fingertips. "I never had much time to teach you when you were growing up," she said. "Not like I did with my first girls." She showed Lizbeth how to pinch the dough to see whether it was ready, before setting it aside to rest.

"Knowing how to rest is what makes us different from the Germans," her mother said, laughing as Lizbeth stood in front of the sink, trying to rub the stippling of dough from her hands.

For a moment, her mother was quiet, watching Lizbeth as though deciding whether to step in.

"All you need is just a little more flour," she finally said and took a pinch from the open bag on the floor and sprinkled it into the cup of Lizbeth's hands. Slowly at first, and then more deeply, her mother rubbed them between her own. Gradually, as Lizbeth watched, the beads of sticky dough began to fall away.

Dandelion Wine

Steep dandelion blossoms in hot water. Let stand 24 hours. Strain. Heat infusion, add sugar and lemons and pour into stone jars to ferment. Skim daily for 6 to 7 weeks before bottling.

The creek was low, a meandering slug trail through a withered garden. Drawn by habit, Joely squatted next to it, dredged up doomed minnows from the muck, and tossed them to a fat tabby that had followed her.

After a month of drought she was bored with the heat, the listlessness that kept everyone doing no more than necessary. Even the chickens laid eggs only in the morning, after which they left the henhouse to doze in the shade.

Joely had hoped her sister would want to help her investigate the hayloft for a new litter of kittens. She knew by the wagging belly of the mother cat that they were up there, but when she crept into Hayley's room in the drape-darkened morning Hayley mumbled something about having only two more weeks to catch up on sleep before heading back to college. Joely climbed up into the loft by herself, but it wasn't the same without someone to help reach shoulder-deep into the scratchy, dark hollows between bales and listen for the faint squeaks of kittens mewing to be fed. After a few attempts, Joely gave up, defeated by the heat, and lowered herself down the wall ladder to the floor of the barn.

The creek smelled of decaying water plants. Only recently, wildflowers, clumps of bluebells and pink asters, black-eyed Susans and wild purple tulips had covered the fields. With summer came mosquitoes and grasshoppers, and only the sturdy yellow dandelions remained, now competing with tenacious wild grasses and prickly weeds to draw up what water there was from the soil. Joely knew plenty of people like that. Resolute, like her mother. But Joely could only ever seem to imitate their resilience. Inside, she felt dormant, waiting for gentler weather to coax her from the dry husk of too many days like this.

Inside the house Joely found her mother basted in sweat, a weekday dress clinging to her skin as she banded and wiped clean a table full of glass jars filled with the overripe apricots she'd cooked down to jam that morning.

Over three sticky days spent in the summer kitchen adjacent to the house, she and Joely had canned preserves, filling rows of sterile jars with the peaches, apricots, and plums they'd bought by the crate from B.C. fresh-fruit trucks. There were still raspberries and cherries to be mashed into sugary red jam, and grapes boiled and strained for jelly.

"Do you think we could go into town today?" Joely said, even though she knew the raspberries probably wouldn't keep another day.

"You can help me with the rest of this fruit is what you can do. Your sister seems to think she doesn't live here anymore," her mother said as she sleeved sweat from her forehead. "She expects me to take jam and crumpets up to her in bed like I'm running some sort of hotel."

Joely hated listening to her mother's complaints, as though it was she who'd asked for buttered brioche and strawberry freezer jam. Joely adored her sister, but that didn't make it any easier to be stuck between her and their mother.

"Our dean makes it for us every second Sunday," Hayley had said one morning, shortly after she'd come home for summer break.

Lately, their mother's mouth tightened whenever Hayley opened hers. "She says there's more to life than white bread and peanut butter."

"Yes, but I don't suppose your dean has a husband, two daughters, and a farm to take care of," their mother said. The girls were eating toast on the porch while she splashed one of two buckets of milk into the separator so they would later have cream for coffee and baking, and butter for bread.

Hayley crushed a grasshopper under the toe of her flip flop. "Oh, Mother."

That was a month ago.

"I guess I'll get the sugar from the pantry," Joely said, estimating how much they'd need to sweeten the eight pails of raspberries picked yesterday from their own overgrown thicket of canes.

"Your dad already brought it to the summer kitchen this morning. If you want, just start sorting the berries and I'll be there in a few minutes. But change your clothes first. And put on an old apron. I'm sure I don't need to spend all night scrubbing berry juice out of good clothes."

Upstairs, Joely found Hayley brushing her teeth. She leaned drowsily against the sink as though being awake was just one of life's inconveniences.

"Hey, babe," Hayley said through a lather of toothpaste when she spotted her sister's reflection in the bathroom mirror.

"Morning," Joely said. She paused in the doorway and admired her sister's figure in crushed cotton boxers and a tank top. There were blanket creases etched into her sister's thighs like pink tattoos.

Everything looked beautiful on Hayley, even sleep, and Joely secretly hoped she'd turn out to look like her sister in a few years, with boyish hips and high, full breasts that filled out sweaters. It was hard to imagine, especially since everyone always said that Hayley matched the women in their father's family, who were tall and lovely and confident. Joely, they said, was more like her mother — built for work.

"We're making jam today," Joely said, hoping she wouldn't have to make another excuse for Hayley.

"What kind?" Hayley lifted a long leg into the bathroom sink and began to smooth thick, white foam up to her knee, flicking it from her fingers onto the counter and mirror before beginning to shave in easy strokes. Joely would end up cleaning the foam later.

"Raspberry, for sure," she said, hoping the mention of her sister's favourite jam would bring her around to feeling helpful. "Mom's already done the apricot with the box that got too ripe for canning. There should be enough to send some with you to school." Joely didn't mention the cherries and grapes. She'd probably already said too much.

Hayley groaned. "Does she expect me to help?"

"I think so. I mean I think she wants us both to." Joely felt an old coal start to burn in her chest and swallowed hard to put it out.

"God, why does all the work have to be done in the hottest week of the whole year? It'll be like the inside of a dragon's mouth in that kitchen when Mom gets all her stockpots boiling." Hayley patted her legs dry with a towel and leaned close to the mirror to examine her face, where a new pimple was threatening under the surface. "Next week will be even worse, you know. She'll want us to pluck chickens. I won't be able to get the smell of scalded feathers out of my hair for days. Oh, well. At least I get to go back to class. Too bad you're stuck here."

"It's okay. You'll be home for Christmas and I'm coming to stay with you for spring break, remember?" Joely was already looking forward to the trip, even though it was eight months away. She was nervous about it though, worried she'd just be a farm bumpkin among all of her sister's sophisticated college friends.

"I know." Hayley yawned, still waking up. "I can't wait for you to meet everyone. I keep telling them what a fantastic little sister I have."

Joely's earlier irritation suddenly lifted like a bit of weather.

"Tell Mom I'll be down in a bit, okay." Hayley shrugged off her top and stepped out of her boxers and into the shower, yelping at the blast of cold well-water.

Meanwhile, Joely changed into frumpy denim cut-offs that made her legs look shorter and wider, and a faded yellow T-shirt with stains on it from last year's jam. She paused at the top of the stairs and closed her eyes in quick prayer for whatever it was God thought she needed, and went downstairs.

"Hayley said she'd help with the jam." Joely brightened the tone of her voice as she entered the kitchen, unsure whether she was telling a lie.

"Good, then," her mother said, her voice flat. She turned and pressed the small of her back against the kitchen counter while she finished eating a Saltine spread with jalapeno jelly. She held out a second cracker to Joely, who wrinkled her nose.

"I don't know how you can eat that," Joely said, scowling at the quivering green glob on the cracker.

"I suppose it's an acquired taste. I didn't always like it," her mother said, eating the cracker in two bites before using her apron to wipe jelly from between her fingers. Her mother had gained weight in the last year. She'd always been somewhat plump, but even with ten new pounds, she still looked underfed. If anything, she appeared sterner. But as Joely watched, her mother's expression began to loosen a little. The furrows between her eyebrows eased. Her shoulders rounded. "The three of us haven't spent enough time together this summer, have we? I don't suppose I'll know what to do if you run off to college, too."

"I haven't decided anything yet." It was the truth. Unlike Hayley, she wanted to stay on the farm, maybe marry someone who'd buy it from her father some day, the way her father had bought it from her grandparents. Still, she wished there could be more to that kind of life than she'd already seen. More than just work and more work. "Besides, that's a long way off still. Two years, almost. And anyway, with all of us working on the jam today, maybe later we'll have time to go into town together."

"We'll see," her mother said, becoming absent again at the sound of lids snapping down as the last of the hot jam jars cooled and sealed. It was important, because anything that didn't seal would have to go into the fridge to use right away, and there'd be less for winter.

"I'll go start sorting berries. They're really good this year. Shouldn't be too many bad ones." Joely turned to leave. Before she could go, her mother stopped her.

"Joely," she said. "I'm sorry. It's just a busy time. Here, I think I have something for you." She opened the fridge and reached to very back of the bottom shelf, behind jars of homemade antipasto, garlic and pepper jellies, marmalade and lime pickle. Un-Mennonite things that didn't fit with the farmer's sausages, homemade noodles and canned chicken that occupied the other shelves. "I always keep something tucked away for days like this." When she stood up, she handed Joely a Snickers bar. "I know they're your favourite, too. We both like nuts, don't we? Now quick, take it to the summer kitchen with you before your sister sees it. I only have the one."

"Thanks, Mom." She gave her a quick hug before slipping away.

Outside, as she peeled back the candy wrapper, she turned to look back at the house, the kitchen window where her mother dipped a small scoop into a box of powdered dish soap that she kept on the sill. It was hard to tell through the warp of old window glass, but to Joely it looked as though her mother was singing.

In the half hour since Joely had last been outside, the heat had intensified and hot breaths of wind flicked at the dust. Joely could feel the beginning of a heat rash pricking her skin and knew it would turn her chest a bright shade of plum. The rash would still be there on Sunday, when she'd planned to wear a floral-print dress that Hayley had given her from her wardrobe. Now she'd have to go to church in her bubblegum-pink blouse that buttoned up all the way to a frilly collar she hated. The blouse was a hand-me-down from a cousin and Joely hadn't been able to grow out of it fast enough. It made her feel like a granny, but at least it would hide the rash.

By the time her mother and Hayley came into the summer kitchen, Joely had sorted through the first three pails of berries. Hayley made a face in the direction of the radio their mother had left playing.

"Change it to whatever you want," their mother said, her mouth withering to a thin line.

"I'll just turn it off," Joely said, knowing that her sister's choice of music would just end up annoying their mother. Hayley would use the term 'lateral move', one of the phrases she had picked up at school and added confidently to her vocabulary. Joely wanted to try out the phrase now, but the words felt clumsy in her mouth.

"How long is this going to take?" Hayley crossed her arms and looked around the summer kitchen, seeming to realize for the first time just how much work there was to be done. "The jars aren't even sterilized yet."

Their mother upended a pail of berries into a stock pot. "Well, if I'd had someone to help me this morning — "

"I'm not going to college to learn how to be a farmer's wife," Hayley said, reaching behind her waist to tie apron strings into a sloppy bow. "In fact, my sociology professor, Judy, says there's no need for a woman in our society to get married at all."

"Tell me that next time you fall in love with some boy," their mother said. But when Joely looked over at her mother, who was stifling a laugh, she knew they were both thinking of her sister's many schoolgirl crushes. The joke was short-lived.

"Oh, Mother. Really. I'm just saying — "

"I know what you're saying. I didn't marry your father because I had no other choice, you know. And you can thank me that I did or you wouldn't be here today to make sure you don't repeat all my old-fashioned mistakes."

"That's not what I meant. I just want to be sure I know why I make my decisions, so they're not based on what society says I should do. And besides, I'm not interested in boys anymore. I'm in college now. They're young men."

Their mother laughed, a sound as dry as paper being crumpled. "Well, let me know if you find one with your modern sensibilities. I can use the money. I've been saving for your wedding to redo the kitchen. I've been thinking it would be nice to paint it peach and put in an island. Maybe even another window so I can get some morning sunlight. What do you think?"

Joely snorted and Hayley, who had been glue-sticking pictures of extravagant gowns and cakes into a scrapbook since she was twelve years old, said, "Fine with me."

They all knew it was a bluff. The wedding fund was sacred to their mother. The last thing she'd spend it on was something for herself. Not when she was known for economizing by filling cracks in the walls with gobs of toothpaste. "It's a trick I learned from your grandmother," she'd say. "Sometimes she had the nuttiest ideas, but they worked." Lately, toothpasting over cracks had become an everyday thing.

"A new kitchen sounds nice," Joely said, playing dumb while getting in a poke at both her mother and sister. When neither replied, she scraped a mound of spoiled berries into a slop pail for the pigs and moved onto the cherries.

The argument fizzled and they turned mutely to sorting and pitting, mashing and macerating, cooking and gelling. They ladled molten jam into hot jars, and loaded jars packed with whole berries into giant pots of water, separating them with old towels to keep them from shivering against each other as the water boiled. Steam filled the summer kitchen and beads of water ran down the windows. When they were finished, their palms were stained with red juice, like the hands of children painting a picture.

"I can't believe we have to do this every year," Hayley groaned once the last jar was wiped and set in a row. "They have jam at the grocery store, you know." Joely knew Hayley wasn't serious. Hayley loved homemade jam, but loved it more when someone else did the work.

"Well, at least it's done for another summer," their mother said. She looked satisfied at being able to quantify their work as she counted the jars and added them to her inventory.

"These ones are for me," Hayley said and quickly claimed six raspberry-filled jars.

"You can take three. And two of everything else."

"Fine," Hayley said, although she returned only two of the raspberry.

"Are we going to do the grapes today, too?" Joely was tired and sticky from the work they'd already done, yet reluctant for them all to go their separate ways. Tension had defined the weeks that

Hayley had been home, but Joely wasn't willing to let it ruin their whole summer.

"The grapes could wait another day, but it would be better to get to them now," their mother said. She looked at Joely, then Hayley, over juice-spattered glasses that had slid down her nose to rest on its tip. She was quiet for a moment as she flapped the hem of her dress to stir up a breeze against her legs. "But I suppose you girls have something better to do."

"I'm not sure what I have planned," Hayley said.

Joely knew what Hayley was thinking — that even if they didn't make the jelly, there was always the possibility their mother would want to try out one of her crazy ideas. Like the year she decided to make chutney out of a bargain box of mangoes she brought home. Or when there were leftover peaches and too many tomatoes in the garden, and she made Hayley and Joely spend a whole day helping to make two kinds of salsa. Or the jalapeno jelly that was last year's experiment, and no one but their mother liked.

"Just wait here a minute until you see what I have," their mother said, lifting the door to the summer kitchen's root cellar and disappearing down under the floor.

"Oh, Mom. Not marmalade," Hayley said when a galvanized milk bucket filled with oranges and lemons was lifted up. "Nobody even likes it."

"Well, I like it. And your father likes it." Their mother was still half buried in the cellar. "If you don't, then go do something else."

"I can stay," Joely said as her mother climbed out and lowered the trap door. She wished she could be more like Hayley who did as she pleased and was already half way to the house. "I've gotten used to the marmalade. I guess maybe it's an acquired taste."

"Yes, well, we're not making marmalade."

"But you told Hayley." Joely pinched her eyebrows together but quickly smoothed them out when she reminded herself what long-term use of a scowl had done to her mother's face.

"Hayley assumed. It doesn't matter, though. She'll be ready another time for what I have in mind. Come on down here with me, I have something to show you."

Confused, Joely followed her mother into the root cellar where it was cool and pleasantly dry, a comfortable contrast to the steam upstairs.

Even though they were underground and the cellar wasn't more than eight feet along each wall, Joely felt able to breathe deeply for the first time since they'd started boiling jam.

Around the walls of the cellar were wooden crates that contained what remained of last year's potatoes and a few bearded carrots, no longer good for anything but the pigs.

"Do you remember your grandmother very much?" her mother said.

Joely hesitated, not sure what her grandmother had to do with anything in the root cellar.

"I remember her a little. She was always busy." She thought for a moment. "But I remember that she laughed a lot, too."

"She did, didn't she?" Her mother grew silent, smiling to herself while Joely waited for her to get to her point. Finally, she said, "The busyness wasn't always just with dishes or dusting. What I remember is that she was always quick to finish her work so she could do things she liked. I've been thinking of her lately. She kept secrets, you know. Sometimes she'd share them with me so I'd know something my brothers didn't."

Joely's mother stepped over to one side of the cellar where a row of shelves lined the wall. They were already beginning to fill up with the overflow of jars of jam and fruit preserves, the pickles from the first cucumbers. All the jars that wouldn't fit in the pantry inside the house. As Joely watched, her mother looked up and down the rows like a librarian searching the spines of books, before she gripped a shelf with both of her hands. "Secrets," she said again. "She gave me this one and I've kept it since your father bought this farm from my father." With a little coaxing, the shelves swung outward like a door, revealing a second, smaller room behind. "This was Grandma's special hiding place."

"For what?" Joely crowded behind her mother to see, feeling suddenly as though she'd been given the key to the Secret Garden from her favourite childhood book. As though everything outside it had somehow become less real. "Did Grandma hide things from Grandpa in here?" Joely felt her heart begin to quicken.

"Secrets are not the same thing as hiding," her mother said, taking Joely's hand and leading her inside. She reached over her head and clicked on a bare light bulb that hung from the ceiling. "But, no, he didn't know about this place. She never told anyone she found it, except for me. This is where your grandmother kept her dandelion wine. And," she said with a pop of a laugh, "where she came to drink it."

"Grandma drank wine!"

"Mm-hm. She taught me how to make it, too, and when she thought I was old enough, about your age, she let me try it."

Joely's eyes grew wide. She could barely believe what she was hearing.

"Did you like it?"

"Not at first. Now, I guess you could say your old mom can be a bit of a lush when she wants to be."

Joely couldn't help herself. She sounded like a goose as laughter forced its way out of her nose as though it was breaking through a barrier. Her mother was smiling and looked pleased with herself.

"But you always do everything you're supposed to," Joely said after she stopped laughing. The were both quiet for a moment. "I always thought I was like you, but you're like Hayley — "

Joely's mother stopped her.

"Both of my daughters are like me. Hayley has more of my adventurous side, although one of these days she might learn to be practical. And you — Well, here." She bent down and picked up a pail and plopped it, full of dandelions, into Joely's hands. "I think you're old enough."

Joely looked around her, taking in the room full of old canning jars that were empty, but for one. She watched as her mother lifted the jar from its shelf. With her apron, she wiped away a covering of dust, revealing pale, amber liquid suspended above a film of silt.

When Joely returned to the house her skin was smudged with yellow, hands sticky with milky resin from plucking dandelion heads off their stems. There was still work to do, adding sugar and lemons and checking on the mixture as it slowly fermented, but, for now, in the hidden pantry, there was a pail of dandelion blossoms steeping in hot water, waiting to be made into wine.

"I was thinking," Hayley said when she came downstairs and found Joely at the kitchen sink washing her hands. "Maybe we should take Mom into town for some girl time. We could have lunch at an actual restaurant instead of just having ham sandwiches between chores."

"She probably doesn't have time," Joely said, paying more attention to the warm water as it fell over her hands and arms.

"Afterwards, we could go to the mall and help her find a new dress so she can throw out that frumpy thing she wears every day. Judy says you can only feel as good as you look."

Joely turned off the faucet and reached for a kitchen towel. Facing her sister she leaned against the counter and patted her skin dry. "Whatever you think. Just ask Mom and let me know what she says."

Loft

Mom didn't know I left the house that morning and followed her, walking on the grass to soften the sound of my footsteps. I hid behind an outbuilding. I hid behind an outbuilding when she approached the barn, squat and solid like a bread hutch. She drew her shoulders back, becoming a little taller before lifting the heavy metal latch with the heels of her hands. After she disappeared inside, I waited a few moments and slipped in after her.

While she preferred to get to the hayloft the easier way, by the ladder in the winter chicken coop, I quietly climbed up through the trap door in the milk room, dust and straw sifting into my hair.

"Elsie?" Mom called up the ladder to you. "Elsie, are you up there?"

It wasn't a real question. Not in the way other questions could be answered with yes or no. You didn't say anything, just pulled yourself farther back between the two hay bales you'd wedged yourself into like bookends, as though your pages were coming loose.

I hid where I could see you sitting with your knees to your chest, as close as you could come to a thick timber Dad had placed to support an unstable rafter above the wall ladder. I knew you would be there. A sister knows.

"Elsie!" It wasn't a question at all anymore. Mom had had enough. Aunt Frances was here to visit us for the weekend. She'd brought her daughters, our city cousins. The ones everyone said were so much more like Mom than we were, with their interest in malls and movies. Mom didn't know what she was supposed to tell them about you, your recent behaviour, the way you kept disappearing. Whatever it was, it wasn't going to be the truth.

Mom was sure you were up in the hayloft and wouldn't leave until she was satisfied. She had seen you steal leftover breakfast toast to feed to the mice, before leaving the house for the barn. But Aunt Frances was with her in the kitchen, sipping tea. She let you go so there wouldn't be a scene. Would she have done the same, I wonder, if she'd known you overheard their conversation that morning?

You knew that feeding the mice made Mom angry. She told you it was like burning money because they ate our grain. They could spread disease. It didn't matter to her that the mice made you smile.

I saw how patiently you sometimes crouched in the hayloft, coaxing a mouse to trust you by holding out a bit of bread. And I knew that once, when you found a mouse still alive, floating in a pail of Mom's dirty kitchen grease, blowing feeble, oily bubbles, you fished it out and hit it on the head with a rock. You were more merciful than the rest of us.

I remember the day Mom caught you doing the same to a kitten from the barn. The kitten was all bones and suffering. So sick its mother had stopped feeding it and moved it away from the others. You were quick. But Mom grabbed you by your shoulders and shook you.

"What's the matter with you?" She yelled and smacked you across the face. I think she surprised herself. After that she went inside the house and bawled. She called Grandma to ask what she should do with you. "I'm just not the right kind of mother for that girl," she said. "She feeds the mice and kills my cats." I guess Grandma didn't have anything to say because nothing changed after that. Except you.

You stopped hiding in the hayloft and started to read books in the kitchen where Mom could see you. You learned to like milky tea instead of the strong coffee you preferred but were too young to drink. You let Mom buy you shoes that couldn't be worn in the barn. You stopped wanting to go to Bible College when you graduated in three more years and started talking about university, a degree that would free you from the farm that you loved. Give you a different future. The one Mom had once wanted for herself before she married Dad and went from being a farmer's daughter to a farmer's wife.

Even though you became what she wanted, Mom didn't trust the changes. She said that it wasn't natural for a girl to turn into someone else overnight. She began to be afraid of what you might do.

I should have told her that you had only changed for her sake. That it was just a garment you'd pulled on, and you were still you. I should have told her something to make her understand. But I didn't. I was too afraid she'd know I was on your side. That she'd start to look at me the same way.

"Didn't you hear me?" Mom said when she appeared at the top of the hayloft ladder and saw you wedged in the hay.

"I heard you," you said quietly. You met her eyes and she thought it was a challenge. If only she had seen how meek you were, how you wanted to please her. Would it have changed what happened?

I understood why you liked to go to the hayloft. The way, when you pressed yourself between the bales, it felt cool and still. You told me it made you feel preserved. Like a jar of apricots in the pantry.

"I don't want to come out just yet. I'm not done," you said. You withdrew a little farther.

"Done what, exactly?" Mom said. She was too far away to reach you and pull you out. Too afraid of you, of the height, to climb over top of the ladder. "Your cousins are here, Elsie, They've been asking about you. Don't you want to come down and see them?" It was a stupid question and she knew it.

"No," you said, hoping to hide that you'd been crying.

"Can I tell them where you are? Maybe they'll want to crawl into some holes, too."

"NO!" You shouted, as though you were years younger than fourteen. You pulled yourself farther into the space.

"Fine, then. Suit yourself. I'll just tell them you've disappeared and that they can check the well to see if you've gone and jumped down it." You were silent for a few seconds. I nearly came out from where I was watching. I was going to tell Mom not to worry, that I'd talk to you. We'd come in together when you were ready.

I stopped when you said, "Go ahead." It wasn't a dare, but it must have sounded like one to her. "They'll believe you."

I should have protected you. The same way I should have come out of my bedroom last night after I heard Aunt Frances tell you, "Just try being cheerful. For your mother's sake." I wish I had been standing there with you. I wish I had stepped between her and you and told her there was nothing wrong with you. That it was only Mom who thought there was. "You don't know what your behaviour is doing to her poor soul," she said. And I did nothing.

You didn't understand what she was asking. How could you? You felt invisible. You just wanted them to see you. Really see you.

Frances was my favourite aunt until that moment. When you came into my room, having given up yours for her, I told you that I was going to start calling her Aunt Fanny, on account of her bigger-than-usual bum. You thought it was unworthy of me. But it made you laugh.

"At least call her Aunt Franny," Mom begged me the next morning. She was spreading jam on toast over lots of butter, the way I'd always liked. "She'd appreciate that. And she meant well, you know. Your sister needs someone to give her some good sense. God knows she won't listen to me."

"I stopped liking jam a long time ago, you know," I said. It was a lie. Although saying so made it true somehow. I haven't eaten jam since.

Mom took one more step up the ladder, as though she might climb over the top, after all.

"You can't stay in the barn all day," she said. And when you didn't reply, "Have it your way. There's no need to do anything for me." You decided to take her at her word rather than her meaning, even though she stayed on the ladder and waited for you to change your mind.

Moments later, we heard our cousins laughing. Megan and Jane; too ignorant to know about anything that didn't come from MuchMusic.

You knew Jane was wearing a pair of pretty ballet-slipper shoes with silk embroidery on the toes. The ones Mom bought you. Mom gave them to Jane when she refused to wear a pair of rubber boots outside, yet complained that her own shoes would get wrecked.

"Here," Mom had said, making sure you saw her disappointment. "Elsie doesn't appreciate them, anyway. Elsie doesn't appreciate any of the nice things I give her."

You liked nice things. Especially the shoes. You didn't wear them often, but when you did I saw the way you touched the silk threads and admired the tiny beads. After a few minutes, though, you'd slip them off, put on rubber boots, and go outside to do your chores.

Once when Meagan and Jane came with Aunt Frances, Jane threw a whole bag full of her old clothes into the nuisance barrel on burning day. They were supposed to be hand-me-downs for you. You were excited about them, but Jane didn't want you to have them, and the only thing she spared from the fire was a sweater. A birthday gift to her from Mom just a month before. Jane pretended she didn't remember. She handed it to you, wrapped in a smoky paper-bag wad, and Mom made you thank her.

"She's probably up a tree somewhere," one of the cousins said. Meagan, I think. Her voice was mocking and shrill. You would have heard her as clearly as I did through the knots and pocks in the floorboards.

"Or in the henhouse with the other chickens." There were peals of laughter.

The cousins had branded you a chicken last winter when, during a game of sixty seconds in the closet, you wouldn't go into the pickle pantry with our all-hands cousin, Andrew. The grown-ups were upstairs cracking nuts. Women in the kitchen, men in the living room. I was old enough to be with the women and saw that even after you told Mom what happened, she sent you back down. Scolded you and told you to start a new game.

Afterwards you blamed yourself, wondering what you expected after agreeing to play when everyone there was related. Except

Todd, our second cousin, who was adopted from some missionary country. He had so much acne that everyone called him Toad. But not you. No one went into the pantry with him even when they were supposed to. When he went in alone you opened the door and told him where to find the sweets Mom kept behind the pickled beets.

Downstairs in the barn, we all heard Megan — it was clearly her — say, "God, this place is so lame." You looked at Mom to see what she would do, but she didn't move. "There's, like, cow shit everywhere. Good thing it matches these stupid shoes!"

"I know. And I don't care what Dad says, either," said Jane. "I'm throwing out everything I'm wearing today after we get home."

"Maybe we should burn it."

They laughed.

Mom looked at you, uncertain.

"Okay, seriously," said Meagan. "Do you think anyone's even seen Elsie all day? I mean she could be dead for all anyone knows, and Aunt Amanda is just in denial or something."

"Yeah," Jane cut in. "Maybe she's hiding the body in the back of the henhouse so she can still visit it and pretend Elsie's the kind of daughter she always wanted."

They didn't know Mom could hear them. I don't think it would have made any difference.

"Did you see Elsie's face when she heard her stupid mother say she'd be happier without her and always having to wonder what she's going to do next? Aunt Amanda didn't even know she was listening."

I saw you listening, Elsie. To Mom that morning from the top of the stairs. To Meagan and Jane in the barn. You didn't know that I told Mom to go after you, told her that you had heard her say those things to Aunt Frances.

"Oh, God," Mom had said when I told her what you heard. "Do you think she'll hurt herself or something?"

"Elsie," Mom said, clinging to the ladder. She was so quiet you could barely hear her. "You know I love you, don't you? Even though you frustrate me sometimes, I love you." She waited for you to answer. Maybe waiting to see whether Meagan and Jane had heard her, too.

It was so little. Nothing, really. But it was enough for you. You crawled out from between the bales and stood. You were about to go to her, but she stopped you.

"No, don't come yet," Mom said, starting back down the ladder. "Come when you're ready. After I'm down." You knew she was so afraid of that ladder, scared that you'd frighten her and she'd fall. Still you forgave her for it.

When she was at the bottom, you went over to the edge and looked down.

I couldn't help it. I wanted to go to you. To step out from where I was hiding and tell you not to trust her. That she'd only disappoint you. I thought you heard me behind you. "Elsie," I said, wanting to protect you. Tell you that it wasn't you who needed to change.

"Elsie." I startled you. I didn't know you didn't see me. When you turned to look I saw you lose your balance. I reached out to pull you back from the edge, grabbing onto the timber to hold us both. And for just a moment before you took my hand, you leaned towards Mom, as though you believed, this time, she would catch you.

MAGPIE

ALL DAY AT SCHOOL MAGDA HAD thought about the news. It crawled around in the front of her mind. Twitched and ate away at her concentration, distracting her from the problems on the chalkboard. Caused her to stare at her hands when she should have been thinking about math, current events, and whether to trade her ham sandwich for Karen Neufeldt's egg salad at lunchtime.

At three o'clock Mr. Toews, her seventh-grade English teacher at the Wymark School, to which she and other village kids were bussed, had called her up to his desk after class to ask if something was wrong. She scowled and lied, saying that everything was "Just peachy, thanks".

Now, standing at the edge of a lane of trees that leads to her grandparents' farm, Magda looks through a screen of leaves at her mother's car. The last time she saw it, or her mother for that matter, was three years ago after Magda's father split and her mother brought her here. Since then, the home where her mother grew up has been Magda's, where she's done her best to forget she ever had parents. Magda feels like stomping in the front door and announcing to her mother that she isn't a sack of laundry. Normal people don't dump off a daughter and expect her to be fluffed and ready whenever they feel like coming back. Yet she can't bring herself to go inside.

When Magda sees her grandfather come out of the house, shield his eyes from the sun with his hand, and squint in her direction, her heart floats into her throat. She swallows it back down and slips round to the other side of the house where there's a carpet of tall grass next to a wooden double-bench swing that her grandfather built for her. She holds her breath and wades in as grasshoppers, hiding in the green coolness, lift up a collective, alarmed rustle with their scabby wings.

The sound would have stopped her once, but not since she was nine years old in Calgary, when her father had figured out that she was afraid of them. After that he took her into their backyard every day and caught the fattest one he could find, making her hold it in her hand until she could stop crying, stop squirming, and finally sit still while the huge insect stared up at her from her palm, daring her, it seemed, to flinch.

"Count as high as you need to," her father would say when they were having one of their grasshopper sessions. "But soon you shouldn't need to go higher than three."

Even at the time Magda knew her father's lessons were meant to toughen her so she wouldn't grow up to be like her mother who, he said, was about as resilient as a bowl of pudding. Her father was more like the spoon, always stirring up the gunk on the bottom.

"I don't know about you, Lizzy," he'd say to Magda's mother when she went to pieces over some small thing. Spilled milk. "You'd think, with what happened to your brother all those years ago, you'd have grown a thicker skin." Her mother would come unglued. Later she'd try hard to put herself back together. And she'd be better for a while.

At the time, Magda didn't know exactly what had happened to her mother's brother, just that it was also why her mother never wanted them to visit the farm in Saskatchewan. Anywhere in Mennonite country was off limits, so Magda's grandparents had always had to come to Calgary for visits.

"There are ghosts back there," her mother said when Magda was still a little girl and asked why.

"Real ones?" Magda said, her eyes wide.

"Of course not. We're still Mennonite, you and me, we don't believe in ridiculous things."

Still, when Magda first arrived on her grandparents' farm she was afraid of what she might find. Even when the only thing was the grasshoppers.

Now, three years later, when they pop up like mustard seeds splashed into hot oil, Magda screws up her nerve and crouches down among them. She cups her hand over a fat yellow insect and carefully enfolds it in the cage of her fingers. She can feel it scrabbling against her skin, probing for a way out. She buries her face into the shelf of her knees, and begins to count.

"One, two, three — "

By now, Magda knows her grandmother will have felt the need to call the school bus driver, who would have told her that Magda was dropped off at the corner of the Wiebes' farm down the road, along with all the other village kids, just like every day. Her grandparents and her mother will know that she's nearby. After all, it's not as though she could hook up with a stranger and hitch a ride into town. There are no strangers here. And no one they know would give her a lift without dropping by and checking with her grandparents first. And that's the other problem. There's nowhere else Magda wants to be.

Above Magda, still holding the grasshopper as it probes against her skin, a canopy of fluttering leaves filters the afternoon sun. She relaxes a little under their shelter.

"Thirty-two, thirty-three, thirty-four — " She looks up when a magpie settles on a telephone wire that intersects the trees, carrying the village's party lines, which is how Mary Dyck, the school nosey-parker, knew Magda's mother had called last night. The little twit had been listening in.

"So is she, like, gonna take you back to Calgary, or what?" Mary had said, giddy and flushed with mock concern, entertainment being otherwise hard to come by.

"I dunno, why don't you tell me? You seem to know more than I do." The truth was, the only thing any of them knew was that Magda's mother was coming.

Magda stopped counting and thought of how her grandfather complained about the party lines that strung the whole village together, two by two, into one big grapevine. "As though anyone around here needs bigger ears."

More than once, though, Magda's grandmother had scolded him for listening. Sometimes he and Magda shared the stool that sat under the old, matte-black wall phone, each with one bum cheek on the seat, and listened together. Usually it was the same old stuff. Church rummage sales, the price of grain, how the prime minister's free-trade deal was giving Canada away to the Americans. Every once in a while they'd get lucky and overhear the pastor of their country church talking to someone far away about his itchy feet, how when he preached on Sundays all he could think about was dropping down behind the pulpit, pulling off his shoes and socks and raking between his toes.

Without meaning to, Magda smiles. But then the smile fades as she thinks of her father. That once, he scolded her for picking up a tarnished ring with a piece of blue, cut glass that she found on the sidewalk in front of their house. He said she was behaving just like a filthy magpie, happy with bits of worthless bits of glitter.

When Magda came to live with her grandparents, her grandfather had called her his little magpie. Then it didn't seem like a bad thing anymore.

"Little magpie," Magda says, losing count. She slides the grasshopper under the toe of her shoe and listens for the popping sound it makes just before its insides squish out.

For nearly half a year after Magda's father took off, she and her mother lived alone in Calgary. Winter came early that year, and by the beginning of November clenched like a fist around their house. At times snowdrifts barricaded the front door so one of them, usually Magda, would have to climb out a window with the shovel and clear a path to the street. But there wasn't much point. Especially when it snowed so much that the schools shut down for an entire week and the city hunkered, frozen and muffled under a thick blanket of snow that replaced itself within an hour of being cleared. During those days her mother couldn't think of a reason to get out of bed.

What Magda remembers most about all that snow is how it dampened the noise of the city, except when someone brave enough to go out would crunch and squeak over it in a pair of winter Sorrels. The sound, which could be heard even inside the house, through the picture window, broke into the silence before it disappeared a little farther down the block.

Insulated as they were, any sounds Magda made seemed magnified. Small clatters bounced off the walls, making it too easy to get on her mother's nerves. And although Magda practiced being silent as though it were a game and noise meant she'd lose points, sometimes she forgot. Or she couldn't help herself. Like if they'd missed breakfast and lunch and it was now suppertime. Instead of swallowing her words to fill her empty stomach, she felt she would burst with them. When she finally spoke, her voice rang out like a dropped dish.

"Maybe we could order a pizza for supper. They deliver so you wouldn't have to go to the store. Or I could go shopping. I could walk," Magda said one evening.

"Oh, for crying out loud, Magda! Don't bother me with that. Just go play in the yard." But it was already after dark and Magda couldn't remember the last time she'd felt like playing. She bundled up anyway and went to sit on the freshly shovelled front steps until her bum was as frozen as the concrete beneath her, and her fingers and toes were like small, frozen potatoes. She waited as long as she could stand to, and a little longer, before she quietly snuck back inside and peeled off her stiffened winter clothes and boots. From there she crept downstairs into the basement, avoiding the creaky fourth and seventh steps. Once at the bottom she opened the door to the cold-storage room which, because its walls were made of cement, stayed nearly as cold as the upstairs fridge. She'd hidden packages of cheese slices and Ritz crackers there, stolen from the last time her mother brought home groceries. And now she took them from the pantry into the warm space under the stairs and, using her old pink-and-white Easy Bake Oven that was a gift from her grandmother when she'd turned six, toasted cheese sandwiches, praying that the smell of hot cheese wouldn't waft up the stairs to her mother.

As far back as she could remember Magda's grandparents had come to visit them in Calgary about twice a year. Usually, just before they arrived was when her father decided he had to go away for work, or visit an old friend who he said needed help. He'd come back, often more than a week later, and act all sorry that he'd missed seeing them. Sometimes he missed them by only a few minutes.

Magda's grandmother had never learned to drive. So whenever she came to the city on her own it was on the Greyhound bus. And for as long as she was there, there'd be lots of good food and the whole house would get cleaned from top to bottom and smell like bleach and baking. Her grandmother kept so busy it was as though she had no 'off' button and never needed to rest, which seemed to have the opposite effect of making her mother grow more and more tired.

"You can't get tired from watching someone else work," Magda had said, more than a little snippily. She was annoyed with her mother for being short with her grandmother who'd spent half the morning cleaning dust and grease from the tops of their kitchen cabinets.

"Wanna bet?" her mother said, looking up from a cup of cold coffee .

If it was a summer visit, and if Magda's grandfather came too, he'd drive Magda to the Co-op a few blocks away. Together they'd thump on huge watermelons, looking for just the right one to go with her grandmother's *rollkuchen*. Her grandmother made a slit in the centre of each rectangle of soft dough and pulled the ends through, so that after they'd fried and puffed up they looked like big doughy bows. *Rollkuchen* with thick, dripping triangles of watermelon was Magda's favourite thing to eat. Especially when she and her grandfather sat outside on the front step and spit seeds onto the lawn.

"Now, don't swallow those seeds, eh?" he'd say. "They'll plant themselves in there and next you'll have watermelons growing in your stomach."

"Are you fooling me, Grandpa?" Magda said. At the time she was still young enough not to know for sure and her suspicion that he might be putting her on was even more delicious than the cold fruit and warm dough.

He laughed through his nose and patted her on her shoulder, said she was a good gurdie.

Things were always best when Magda's grandparents were around. Even so, after it had been months since Magda's father left them for that last time, her mother told them they shouldn't visit for a while. And no, she didn't know when would be a good time. Maybe next year. Maybe never.

"We're fine here alone," her mother said, her voice a wound-up spring. "There's no reason I can't take care of myself and my own daughter."

"Why won't you let them come?" Magda said afterwards, her fingers fisted together.

"What, and take care of us? Are we so helpless without your father? When did he ever do anything for us? Tell me that."

"At least when he was here you tried to cook and keep things nice." Magda looked around at the mess that had gradually begun to crowd in on them. "Well, I want Grandma and Grandpa to visit. Or doesn't anything I want matter?"

"Yeah, well, maybe I should send you to live with them," her mother said. She took a step forward and stood over Magda, but instead of looking larger as was the usual effect, her mother suddenly seemed smaller and far away.

"Great. When do I leave?"

From her hiding place in the tall grass Magda listens to her grandfather's footsteps as he comes near. He's looking for her and it takes all of Magda's resolve to keep from revealing herself to him.

When she first came to live with them, Magda used to disappear for hours at a time. There were endless places to hide on the farm. After a while her grandfather would always come looking. He was good at knowing where she'd be and seemed able to see her through anything.

"Why don't you just leave me alone?" she said whenever he found her and, with creaky knees, slid down to sit beside her on the ground against whatever outbuilding had been her shield.

"Why would I do that?"

"I dunno. Maybe because I don't want to be found." But as many times as she'd hidden and as many times as she said things to make him want her gone, her grandfather never stopped finding her. Eventually she had stopped trying to hide.

Even now, although she's crouching as still as she can in the grass, she's sure her grandfather can see her. Especially when that stupid magpie flies off the telephone line above them and lets out a shrill laugh as if to tattle on her. She'd like to throw a rock at it, strike it right out of the air, but she'd give herself away for sure.

Magda can hear her grandfather take a deep breath, like a slow drink, and let it out. She knows he's looking at the sky, appreciating the beautiful day. He always does, even when it's not.

"She'll come home," her grandfather says to himself, loud enough for Magda to hear. His voice is gentle and sure and Magda has never understood how he can be so calm when the sky is falling. Literally. Like when it hails and he doesn't even get uptight about all the crops that are being ruined.

He waits there a few moments longer, just feet away, until Magda thinks he's going to wade into the grass and crouch down with her. But he turns back towards the house and walks away, leaving Magda to decide whether to follow.

When her grandfather is gone, Magda gets up and goes round to the other side of the trees, her feet fat and numb from squatting so long. Soon, though, she feels the thousands of pinpricks of blood rushing back into her tissues, as though she's walking on a pair of her grandmother's tomato-shaped pin cushions.

Behind the grass and trees, hidden from the house, is the garden. Really it's two gardens. There used to be a fence between them but it was taken down when, a long time ago, her grandparents bought the house next door to theirs and used it to store old furniture, tools, and potatoes. It's a rickety old building that wouldn't be good for living in anymore, but Magda likes it, even though she knows, now, that the people who once lived there were responsible for what happened to her mother's brother. He had brought a Bible over to talk to them and was shot dead for it later while he worked in the garden. Afterwards, her grandparents wanted to make sure they'd never have to worry about neighbours again.

"Your mamma was so broken-hearted," Magda's grandfather told her when she asked about that time. "It was as though we buried two children instead of only one."

But Magda doesn't care how her mother felt. She thinks she should've gotten over it by now.

As Magda stands in the garden she wonders if she'll be here to help with the harvest this year when her grandfather turns over the potato mounds with a pitchfork. He always pays her a nickel for every ice cream pailfull she empties into a wheelbarrow, which he takes to the root cellar in the old house.

Although they're not the prettiest plants in the garden, Magda likes the potatoes. Even when the prairie winds scrape over them, the plants are both sturdy and flexible enough that they'll bend without snapping. It would take one storm after another to lay them down.

For a while, after threatening to send Magda away, her mother made an effort to improve things for the two of them. She filled the fridge and pantry with groceries and spent time every day in front of the stove, an open recipe book next to her on the counter. During the day she listened to gaggingly uplifting music and hummed as she tidied the house, scrubbing places she'd never scrubbed before, like under the fridge. She bought a cheery plant for the kitchen windowsill, an African violet that she watered every day. She fussed over Magda too, hovering to make sure she was keeping up with her homework, asking whether she was happy. Although Magda wanted to trust the change in her mother, she could practically feel the ground shifting beneath them.

"Molly and some friends are going to the mall today. Can I go with them? Her mom's driving," Magda said one Saturday when the calendar said it was spring but the weather didn't agree.

"Of course you can." Her mother clucked like a fretful hen as she reached into her purse and handed Magda five dollars. One of many little love bribes that she'd handed over lately. "I want you home early though, so I'll pick you up by the Yogen Früz at four o'clock sharp. Don't be late, okay, honey?" Calling Magda honey was part of the whole happy charade, too.

"Sure, whatever — I mean, thanks. Really."

For two hours Magda and her friends roved from store to store, giggling and trying on new clothes. Everywhere they went they were watched closely by suspicious sales clerks who had no patience for anyone under twenty. But the girls didn't care. It only made it more fun to have an audience when, with mock despair, they lamented their too-big bums or breasts that refused to grow, even though there were girls in their class whose had. Just before four o'clock Magda finally spent her money on a large Coke from the food fair, and a T-shirt that she found in a discount bin.

"The mall doesn't even close until five," Molly said when Magda announced that she had to go meet her mom. Molly was relatively new to Magda's school and had become instantly popular for her hair that was the colour of fresh beeswax and always looked as though she'd just had it cut, and for the way she made faces behind the teachers' backs and always got away with it.

"Yeah, but she'll freak if I'm not there."

"Whatever. But you're missing out," Molly said to Magda's back as she hurried towards the Yogen Früz, the ice in her Coke rattling against the cup.

"Crap," Magda said under her breath when her mother wasn't there. If there was anything she and her mother had in common, it was that they hated to be kept waiting.

Magda plonked down on a mall bench and, for the next fifteen minutes, jiggled her foot impatiently. She glowered at the glass doors until her mother was half an hour late. "C'mon, c'mon, c'mon, c'mon, c'mon," she said under her breath, looking at her watch every few seconds. "Okay, now. Okay, now," she said, over and over, after it had been forty-five minutes. She blinked hard and willed her mother to magically appear every time she opened her eyes.

When she finally did show up it was five past five and the mall was closing.

"Have you been here long?" her mother said. Her voice was high and sweet but she was flustered.

"Yes!" Magda said, standing up. "Where have you been?"

"I got busy at home. Besides, I thought you'd like a little extra time with your friends. Did you have a good afternoon?"

"How could I have a good time? You told me to be here at exactly four o'clock and I've been here since exactly four o'clock." Magda waved her arms. "Now I'm starving."

"Don't you raise your voice at me," her mother said, a whisper ground to an edge. "I gave you five dollars. Why didn't you buy yourself a yogurt? You're not the only one who matters here, you know. You think I wanted to come pick you up today? I have enough to do and think about without you always wanting something from me."

"I didn't want you to pick me up. I could've come home with Molly."

Magda's mother pinched Magda's arm hard and started to pull her towards the door, where Magda could see that the car had been left running. She twisted herself free before they got there and stomped away in the opposite direction. When she looked back, expecting to see her mother coming after her, she found that she had left. When Magda walked into the house an hour later, soaked to the shoulders with wet snow, neither of them said anything.

The next day, the flowers fell off the African violet in the kitchen window. Magda's mother packed up Magda's things and they drove to her grandparents' farm, six hours away and as far removed from the life Magda knew as if they'd driven to the moon.

"It's not your fault, Magda. It's not you. I just can't do it anymore, not alone," her mother said, words spilling from her mouth when they finally turned onto the gravel driveway that led to a white farmhouse with black trim. "Just — just promise me you won't be too happy with them, okay?" She bit her lips as she pulled up to the back door, shifting the car into 'park' a moment too soon. The car rocked to a stop as Magda's mother grabbed one of Magda's hands in hers and pressed it to her face, which was hot and damp. Magda knew her mother wanted her to cry too, wanted it to be something they did together. But Magda just looked out the passenger window and thought about grasshoppers.

The first spring that Magda lived with her grandparents, her grandfather gave her a new pair of gardening gloves and a watering pail filled with shiny new hand tools: a spade, a weeder, and a trowel. The three of them went down to the garden and planted flowers. With seeds from last year's blooms, they filled in rows that were roped off with her grandmother's kitchen string. There were petunias and sweet peas and marigolds which, when they finally bloomed, nodded their heads in the breeze. Everywhere else in the garden were sensible pickling cucumbers and carrots, radishes, green onions, kohlrabi, peas, musk melons, strawberries, and prickly canes of raspberries. The garden was like a patchwork quilt, with the flowers, Magda learned, covering the place where her uncle had died. When the sweet peas were tall enough, Magda helped train them to grow up kitchen-string trellises, until they became a screen of colour.

Now when Magda wanders through the rows of flowers, she picks the pink and purple sweet peas that look like little lips. She litters the soft petals behind her as she walks. When she comes to the marigolds she pulls the nearest plant up by the roots, some of which gets torn away and left behind in the soil.

Magda pushes the plant back into place. She wonders what will become of it now, whether it will be able to root itself again. She brushes her hands on the thighs of her jeans, leaving soiled handprints, and begins to kick her way through the rows of vegetables, feeling a constriction of guilt over ruining her grandparents' careful work. Yet she knows they won't be angry with her.

"Doesn't it make you sad to use this garden?" Magda said to her grandfather once, when they were weeding between the rows of green beans.

He stopped and leaned on his hoe, bobbing his head as he looked around. "Your grandma and I, we've forgotten what happened here," he said. "And the Lord, He has forgotten, too."

"What does that even mean?" Magda scowled, chipping at a clod of dirt with her hoe. "You're remembering it right now."

He was quiet for a moment. "It means we choose not to remember."

"Well, whatever. God might forget," Magda said. "But people don't. They just leave."

"*Miene dochta*," he said a little sadly. "Look at these beans you helped me plant." He bent over and plucked a slender, green pod. "See, you have to pick them so there's room for new ones to grow. Some day, I think, you will know how to forget, too."

Standing alone in her grandparents' garden, Magda knows it's just a matter of time before she'll have to return to the house and face her mother. As she turns to go, she finds her grandfather sitting on the bench swing he built for her, next to the grass she had tried to hide in.

Magda breathes as deeply as she can and lets out a long, uneven breath. "Has she come to take me away?" Magda says. She sits next to her grandfather on the swing. He smells like *rollkuchen* from her grandmother's kitchen.

"I don't know," he says, taking her hand and holding it tight.

"It's not up to me, is it?"

Her grandfather is quiet for a while, nodding his head in quiet thought.

"Some things are up to you."

Undone Hero

Inside the kitchen cupboards of the farmhouse, pots are stuck to the shelves, cemented with condensation as cold seeped through the hundred-year-old sawdust insulation.

Leaning against the sink, Alec listens to the storm. Even the air in the house has begun to stir as wind finds its way in through cracks that have opened up around windows and doors. The gas has been turned off since his father stopped paying bills and the wood burning fireplace isn't able to keep up.

If Alec's mother were alive, she would use her hair dryer to shrink-wrap the windows in winter plastic. Without her, the musty old curtains swell softy and go flat. The whole house bends to the wind and hunches under the weight of snow.

"If I ever start shitting myself, you just take me out back and shoot me, eh?" his father says from his chair in the living room. "Better to go to hell a little early than be stuck here in my own shit." He has tried to make this pact with Alec dozens of times over the years. But where it used to sound like a threat, now there's a tremble in his father's voice.

"Yeah. You already know I won't do that, Dad."

His father reaches down beside him for his cane and thwaps the floor with its crook, showing more strength than Alec thought he still had. Enough perhaps, to keep on this way for weeks.

"I'm not going to any home, whatever you have in mind. You make sure I'm good and dead before they come to take me away. You do it. That sister of yours can't be trusted."

"She's not coming, Dad. You know that."

"Good. Don't need her," he says. "Don't need anything." He leans back in his chair and presses his head into the rotten upholstery.

Yesterday Alec called to tell his twin sister. Just in case she might want to make peace before their father dies. Cassandra however, is staying in Winnipeg, uninterested in revisiting what she thinks she dealt with years ago.

Selfish, Alec thinks. If not for Dad, or herself, then — He pushes the thought aside.

"Why don't you bring us both something for the pain, eh?" Alec's father says, coughing out each word.

"Sure, Dad. Why not?"

"Why not is right. And hey — " He spits and conceals the bloody phlegm inside a handkerchief. "We'll toast that sister of yours. Don't need her anyway."

"You already said that, Dad."

"Yeah and it goes double. Just like the drink you're gonna pour me."

Alec spins his wedding ring on his finger. He'd have brought his father home with him to Saskatoon, but the last thing he needs is a crotchety old man to teach his three-year-old daughter, Allison, how to swear. And besides, his father is determined to be right where he is. It would be easier to turn a stone into bread than get him to budge. The same is true of Cassandra.

Even when Alec and his sister were younger, Alec stayed at home until he finished college, driving an hour into the city every day while Cassie ran off the first chance she got. And now, here he is again, back after the hospital called to say his dying father was demanding to be released and was there someone in the family who could come and get him? Who else but him? Who else would know his father keeps his liquor under the sink behind the Drano.

Alec fills a glass two fingers high with cheap Scotch and carries it back to the living room. His father's sour breath has frozen on the window, near where he's tucked in up to his chest under a heavy quilt. The layers of frost are uneven and bend and shift images on the other side of the glass into a relief that's almost beautiful.

"What? My liquor not good enough for you?" his father says, taking a long, grateful snort.

"I don't drink, Dad."

"Ha. Just like your mother," he says. "I knew there was something I didn't trust about you. Next you'll be wanting me to get on my knees and beg that God of yours for mercy before I die."

Alec sits down in his mother's favourite reading chair and pretends to listen to his father's rant, wondering whether the old man has been to the toilet. It would be just like him to wait, no matter the agony. He'd wait until Alec went to bed, even though he's not supposed to get up on his own. Which he must have done last night. Because, if nothing else, he's at least clean.

"I'll guar-an-tee you this," his father is saying. Guarantee. The first 'a' pronounced like the 'a' in arsenic. Garr-an-tee. The way he says it has always made Alec want to turn and shout "Guarantee, Dad! It's pronounced guarantee." But Alec never did, and his father kept repeating himself until someone paid attention.

"What, Dad? What do you guarantee?" Alec says, making sure to pronounce the word correctly.

"That a man can only ever count on his son, that's what." He shrinks back into his chair. When he goes on, his voice is a blunt edge. Alec remembers how it once seemed sharp enough to cut spirit from flesh. "Can't count on women. Where are they when the chips are down?" His mind has drifted and he isn't speaking to Alec anymore. "Off getting something for themselves. Even my Carol's gone and deserted me."

Alec looks into his father's face, its wrinkles that weren't there even last year, now covered with a three-day bristle of white-and-grey whiskers.

"Dad," Alec says. "Mom died. She didn't leave you."

"Your father's a good man, Alec. He just doesn't know it," Alec's mother had sometimes said.

And there were days. Like when he bought Alec and Cassie toboggans for their seventh birthdays, and before the kids could get themselves stuffed into their snowsuits, was already at the door waiting for them. He was more excited than they were, which was almost better than presents.

All morning, their father helped them drag the toboggans up a hill at the back of their property. He waited until both kids were ready and gave Cassie, then Alec, a mighty push before jumping on the back of Alec's sled and riding down with him. Up and down. Dozens of times, each time breathlessly fun, right up until the end.

After what turned out to be the last run, Dad sat in the snow at the bottom of the hill and Alec watched as his expression clouded over. By the time they trudged back to the house all three of them were caked in snow and exhausted. While the kids stood in the porch, peeling off their damp parkas and snow pants, their father went to the bedroom he shared with their mother and shut the door.

Just before supper, when the food, which had been prepared in silence, was taken from the oven and brought to the table, Dad's door opened. When he sat at the table he was so quiet that all the sound in the room seemed to have been swallowed. He didn't appear angry. Yet, Alec knew that he had spent all that time behind his door thinking hard thoughts.

"Mommy and I made tuna noodle casserole," Cassie said. She always said Mommy or Daddy instead of Mom and Dad when she was anxious.

Alec looked in his father's direction to show he was paying attention and not thinking about eating, even though he was starved and worried that his stomach would start to rumble and betray him. But he accidentally met his father's eyes. He was trapped.

Alec knew that staring back was seen as a challenge. Yet, looking away was an admission of guilt to whatever it was his father thought he'd done. So he couldn't look away, but if he'd had a clear shot he sure would've kicked Cassie under the table to make her stop squirming.

Before he spoke, Dad took a deep breath. "You two think I'm some kind of Santa Claus."

Silence.

"You know that's not true," Alec's mother said, spooning tuna and noodles onto Dad's plate.

"No? Well maybe we should start with the fact that these two didn't even think to say thank you for those goddamn toboggans, or for my dragging them up that goddamn hill all morning."

On cue, Cassie began to cry. Softly, at first, but then in hiccupping sobs until she could no longer catch her breath. Pathetic.

"Look what you've done," Mom said. "The kids are plenty grateful for those sleds. They've talked about nothing else since coming in but what a wonderful time they had out there with you." But that's as far as she went. She wrung her frustration into a damp tea towel and led Cassie from the table to help her calm down.

Alec didn't move from his chair, expecting that once they were alone his father would go on with his tirade. Dad pounded his fist on the table, once, and glowered at his noodles. Eventually he lowered his face into his hands and shook his head. He got up and left the kitchen, leaving Alec to wonder whether he was allowed to eat.

Now, what feels like a hundred years later, Alec wonders if his father still remembers that day with the toboggans. How, when he and Cassie were older and their mother gone, they were just supposed to know when they were expected home after being allowed to visit a friend. It was the same kind of test as the staring. If they arrived too early, Dad assumed they were guilty of something. Too late, and they must be trying to push their limits, which would quickly get snapped back until there was no slack left in the rope.

There was only ever a ten-minute window of correctness and Alec became expert at climbing through.

Cassie though, never did figure out when to come home.

"You need a nurse to visit," Alec says as his father lapses into another fit of coughing. "They said your lungs would fill up."

"No-ho!" he says, catching scraps of breath and using them to expel his voice, together with drops of spittle. "You know what I said about that. When it's my time I'm ready to go, damn it! Just get out of here if you aren't going to help me. Or do me in like a good son." With his fingers shaking he uses his next breath to light a cigarette.

Alec looks up as though God might be in the ceiling, but sees only flaking paint and rotted wood, frozen drops of water from where the heat of the fire meets the cold of the rest of the house. Smoke rises from his father's chair, covering him with grey gauze.

In the years since Alec and Cassie's mother died, Dad's bitterness had slowly eroded any gentleness that once existed. He stopped going to the Mennonite Brethren Church in the nearest village, but insisted Alec and Cassie stand at the end of their driveway every

Sunday morning, no matter the weather, to be picked up by their nearest neighbours and ferried to Sunday School.

Back in the kitchen, Alec lifts a blackened pot from the sink. The oats he left in it from breakfast have bloated and the pot is beginning to gather frost around its edges, like the pond outside would have done sometime back in October. The same pond Alec and Cassie used to float waxed-paper boats on after the summer rains, when there were any. And where in a different November, they watched a flock of late-migrating Canada geese land, skidding on unexpected ice before their bodies splashed down into the unfrozen centre.

By morning the geese were all on the shore of the pond, eating their fill of wilted greens. All but one. An albino goose, eerily white, was frozen in the centre of the pond, its pink eyes wild with panic and wings beating the ice.

Alec and Cassie, who always woke early to fresh snow, had spilled outside, unable to delay their play another moment. But then they'd heard the terrible honking and arrived at the pond to find the goose there, its flock unconcerned and eating.

Seeing the children, the white goose hissed and flapped its wings to reveal a hem of bloody feathers where the ice had cut into its legs. A moment later it slumped onto the ice and was still.

Cassie grabbed Alec's arm and shook it. "Do something!"

When he tested the ice, it was too thin to walk on or even to crawl on for very far. Cassie was frantic, always soft when it came to the suffering of animals. So Alec ran and pulled his toboggan out of the shed, tied a rope to the curl of wood in front and pushed himself out towards the bird while his sister held limply to his lifeline and sobbed into her scarf.

Alec inched towards the goose, moving himself and the sled by pulling and pushing against the ice with his gloved fingers and toes of his boots.

The ice creaked and groaned under his weight and Alec closed his eyes as he struggled forward. When he opened his eyes again, he had covered most of the distance and was nearly knocked unconscious as the goose reared back and flapped its wings against his head. Although his heart pounded against the make-do raft, Alec's hands were steady as he retrieved from his pocket a hammer that he'd thought to grab from the shed. He began, delicately, to knock the ice from around the bird's imprisoned legs. As he did, water soaked through his gloves and the sleeves of his coat, but he kept working, wet and freezing, all the time wondering how a coyote or badger hadn't already had its way with this creature during the night. There should have been nothing left for him and Cassie to find but a mess of guts and bloody feathers and two gnawed legs trapped in the ice.

"Be careful, Alec." Cassie sniffled and sobbed at the edge of the pond, where she stood rooted, still loosely holding onto the end of the rope.

"Get ready to pull!" Alec shouted, his voice shuddering with cold as his muscles began to lose control. "I need you to help." And with that he tapped the ice one last time and braced himself for it to fracture and for the goose to whack him senseless as it took off into the air.

The ice merely collapsed in a sheet under Alec's weight. Water rushed over the toboggan and soaked his chest and legs. The goose crumpled, wings open on the water, too exhausted to act on its unexpected freedom. Alec dragged the goose up next to him on the toboggan, and with the last of his strength turned them around and tugged on the rope that connected him to the shore.

Cassie was still blubbering as she turned away from the pond and put the rope over her shoulder, letting Alec pull against her until he was close enough to shore to crawl, dragging the goose the rest of the way. Cassie left him there, dripping, and ran home to wake their mother.

"There they are! It's not my fault; I didn't make him do it!"

Mom was furious with both of them. Years later, Alec would understand that her anger was mostly fear. At the time he was simply relieved to let her wrap him in a blanket and help him to the house, drops of goose blood forming a trail behind him.

"Do you know what could've happened?" she said. "What would we do without you?"

"I had to get the goose," was all he said. And without scolding him again his mother lifted the large bird from his arms, its head dangling at the bottom of its neck, and carried it into the house with them. She sent Alec upstairs to a warm bath and busied herself, with Cassie's now-cheerful help, reconstructing their old playpen from the attic, where it had been since they were babies. She smeared ointment on the goose's wounds and set it inside the pen on top of an electric blanket. She lit a fire and pushed the goose close enough to catch the heat.

"Remember that goose?" Alec asks his father, emerging from the kitchen with a mug of black coffee. He sets it on a television tray for his father if he feels up to it.

"Would've been a fine feast if all of you hadn't blubbered over it the way you did."

"After everything we did to save that thing, I couldn't believe you wanted to cook it."

"Bird was half dead when you brought it in. A mercy to finish it off instead of letting it go on suffering like that."

"Probably."

That night Cassie had announced her plans to keep the goose as a pet and walk it on a leash. She went off to bed happy while

Alec carried a blanket downstairs and was kept awake worrying over the way it didn't seem to care about being caged.

"Your mother was as soft as the both of you," Alec's father says. "Three peas, the three of you."

"Three peas," Alec says, a smile fleeting across his face for the only time since the hospital called. "Have you taken your pills today?" he asks, reaching for the box of bottles, knowing the answer is no.

"Don't need that poison," his father says, gumming the insides of his cheeks without the teeth he says were stolen in the hospital. "Doctor's trying to kill me with those. Ask your mother. She knows the truth."

"Mom's not here, Dad. She's gone," Alec says. His father nods as the truth sinks back in.

In the night, Alec slips downstairs from his old room, where a plug-in oil heater has created a capsule of warmth around his bed, and adds a log to the fire next to where his father sleeps in his chair. Later, Alec allows him the dignity of finding the bathroom by himself, although this time Alec hears what a struggle it is for the man who has always prided himself on stubborn strength above everything else. When he comes out of the bathroom, Alec is outside the door and helps him back to the living room where he collapses in his chair and pats Alec's hand before letting go. After sitting with him through the rest of the night, Alec is ready with breakfast before his father wakes.

"I've had oatmeal every morning my whole life," his father says. "That stuff'll keep you alive forever."

Alec snorts. His father's smoked for more than fifty years. He replaced Bible reading with drinking when he was widowed. Now his liver is soaked in alcohol, his lungs are coals. But the oatmeal. Yes, the oatmeal will save him.

The goose rallied in the night, thumping its wings on the floor of the playpen until it got to its feet. After that Alec was able to sleep. By morning the bird was dead.

"We're lucky to have such a strong father," Alec said to Cassie when she was fourteen and said she was going to leave. Their mother's sister had agreed to give her a room in exchange for help around the house.

"He's strong, all right," she said, her hand covering a bruise on her arm where Dad had grabbed her to make her listen to one of his speeches.

"He's sorry. I can tell. He won't do it again."

As Alec considers the man who has been reduced to his chair, he wishes he had never tried to apologize for him. It wasn't the first time he was rough with Cassie. Just the first time Alec let himself see it.

Alec gently wraps a scarf around his father's neck and listens to him breathe. The gas company was supposed to be by to turn the heat back on yesterday, but so far they haven't arrived, just cashed the cheque he gave them to cover the arrears and a month in advance.

"Do you want a Christmas tree, Dad?" Alec asks. He's been thinking that it might be nice to have the lights to look at at night.

"It's barely the middle of November. What do you think, I'm gonna die before it's even Christmas?" Alec's father looks at him, then away. "Don't need no damn tree in here, but you do what you want."

"Okay, Dad. I'll see what I can find."

By noon, the gas company has come through the storm, the pilot on the furnace has been relit and the smell of its first breath of fuel is a not-unpleasant, sleepy smell in the house. By three o'clock, drips of water fall from the ceiling, raining onto the furniture and floor. Alec's father lets him move him a few feet farther from the fire where it's dry. Alec sits down on the floor by his father's feet and rests a hand on his hospital slipper.

"Your sister," his father says. "Cass — "

"Cassandra, Dad," Alec says.

"Your sister always liked Christmas. Too much. Always wanted more presents. A father shouldn't have to be Santa Claus, you know. There's other things a father needs to be."

"Like what?" Alec asks, leaning forward to make his father face him. "Like what, Dad?"

Year of the Grasshopper

So MANY GRASSHOPPERS THAT YEAR, ENOUGH that two or three were found clinging to the head of each stalk of wheat in the fields. And not enough poison in the country for even Saskatchewan to be rid of them. A farmer might as well have fired birdshot into his crops for all the good it would do to spray. Or sent my brothers to pull the insects' legs off, crippling them, so when they snapped their wings they'd fall back to the ground, unable to achieve flight without the advantage of hop.

There was a time when I was very young that I might have thought this cruel, but I came to hate the insects so feverishly that, years later, when there were only a few, I'd cross the street to avoid a grasshopper on the sidewalk.

That year the country was choked with them, their smell like burnt hair. Sunsets were blacked out, voices of birds swallowed by the noise of a swarm that single-mindedly ate as one.

I was an ignorant child and didn't understand why my grandpa and uncles stood clench-fisted as their work was devoured, when they prayed for relief, and when it didn't come, for faith.

I didn't need to visit the farm; I might have stayed in town with my mom and played inside the house. But I'd have missed petting the friendly barn cats as they sunned their fur and lazily swatted the occasional grasshopper out of the air. And I wouldn't have been able to help my grandpa with his chores or go with him in his big Ford truck that smelled sweetly of manure and hay, to count cows in the summer pasture. Whenever I walked with my grandpa, the grasshoppers would jump out of the way in front of us, as though the path was being peeled.

I rode in the grain trucks and combine too, during the harvest of what was left, and held my breath to keep from panicking whenever a grasshopper flung itself through an open window and pivoted to look at me with its black-bead eyes. My grandpa grinned — his face wrinkled and bristly with white whiskers — as he reached over to pinch it dead and pop it back outside.

After what little grain there was was spilled into the auger — a dangerous machine that I was never allowed near — I rode an old-fashioned bicycle up and down the gravel road through Schoenfeld, my grandparents' village. I spread my arms and legs, pretending they were wings, and laughed when the grasshoppers parted in front of the wheels.

This was the first summer I went to visit my other grandparents who lived a hundred miles away in Fox Valley, where there was no valley and I didn't see any foxes.

Some things — the grasshoppers, the stunted quilts of wheat they fed on — appeared the same, but everything that mattered was different. My new grandparents had ways of doing things that made me feel small and underfoot. They didn't need my help.

One morning, I followed my new grandfather, expecting to go with him out to the fields, but he left me on the porch and drove away. I noticed that the grasshoppers didn't part for him, but were crushed under his boots when he walked. And when he drove his truck through them, they stirred up into a storm.

As I stood on the cement steps the grasshoppers began to settle. The insects he'd trampled twitched, their legs stirring through their yellow eggs and entrails. My feet felt glued to the porch. I pictured myself taking a step, pulling away from the imaginary adhesive, which would stretch like gum between my shoe and the cement. Then down the three stairs, while the bones in my legs jellied.

I closed my eyes and tried to make the scene turn out differently, the way my first grandpa seemed able to make the grasshoppers move aside, the way they parted in front of my bike. With my fingers rolled up into fists I took one step, another, and another.

The nearest grasshoppers tensed, squat with readiness to jump. But instead of letting me through they sprung up and snapped their wings, thousands in every direction, dipping and swerving erratically with each stroke. The nearest ones pitched themselves against my legs and scrabbled to cling to my bare skin with their spiny elbows. More grasshoppers replaced them as they fell away. Others latched onto my socks and the hem of my shorts, shuffling their wings closed under their scabby backs. They stared up at me, their eyes hard, mouths miming the action of devouring. I took another step and, trying to brush the insects away, only excited more of them to spatter against me, land higher and higher against my waist, my back, my chest. They grasped and scraped their way over my arms and shirt, into my shorts, under my shirt and into my hair. I looked in the direction my grandfather had gone but knew, in this place, I was alone.

Poor Nella Pea

MY MOTHER'S HOUSE IN SWIFT CURRENT has belonged to me for six months. This is the first time I've been home since she died.

In January, rather than sort and box all the memories that exist as shelves of chipped curios, antique linens and decades of clothes, I simply locked up and left. The only thing I took was my mother's childhood diary, my other inheritance. It's paperboard cover is swollen and tattered now, from being read while I washed dishes, and being dropped in the rain.

The house too, has deteriorated. The original wooden front steps have bowed even deeper for not being shovelled all winter. And the whole structure leans more to the left, away from the prairie wind.

I climb the worn, arthritic steps up to the porch and discover that one of the front windows is broken, probably by a neighbourhood boy throwing stones. I pick up the larger pieces of glass that have sheared from the rotted frame and set them on the porch rail.

There are other small vandalisms, too. A pair of lover's initials carved into the crumbling paint behind a plastic loveseat — an addition of my father's that never sat well with my mother. And hanging from her unpruned rosebushes, which stubbornly insist on blooming year after year, are banners of toilet paper which, having been rained on and dried in the sun, drape like papier mâché ghosts across the thorny branches.

The front lock still requires some finesse, calculated jiggling and a specific click like a password for gaining access to a club. Once the door is open I step over the splintered threshold and instinctively turn out the porch light, left burning all this time. Even though everyone in the neighbourhood knows that the old yellow house bordering the CPR line has been empty these months, leaving a light on at night is still what people around here do to let everyone know someone's home, whether they are or not.

I expect to find that the mice have moved back in. All through my childhood they'd always found ways, no matter how many holes were boarded up on the outside. And now, judging by the trail of droppings along the floorboards, they've made themselves at home.

Except for a thick film of dust, everything else is as it was. Heavy drapes are drawn across the windows, the furniture arranged not for comfort, but as props. The thirty-year-old lampshades still wrapped in their original cellophane.

After a walk-through of the main floor, trying to appraise it as a buyer might, I take the staircase to the second storey. The banister is so thickly waxed it feels like a candle, and when I touch it, dust sifts down around the spindles like silt settling in a pond after it's been churned up. It's going to take a lot of work to scrape away all the evidence of the lives lived here. Much more though, my realtor says, if I want to sell the house rather than pay someone to push it over.

Upstairs in my parents' bedroom, there is more damage. Beads of moisture have collected under the windowsill, some calcifying over the years into little, rounded stalactites which, when I touch them, feel like calluses. Early last spring, when Mom complained of a draft — there had always been drafts — my father carefully caulked all the seams. But no amount of sealing was enough to keep the house from losing what little heat the ancient furnace in the basement was still able to breathe out. Cold has always seeped in through the single-paned windows. And now that my father has gone willingly, maybe even gratefully, into a retirement home, there's no one left to care for the house but me.

This room never suited my mother. The walls and switch plates are papered with an insistently cheerful, thornless, yellow-rose pattern chosen by my grandmother when the house belonged to her. Mom inherited the wallpaper more than fifty years ago, along with the heavy dressers which, if moved, would reveal dents in the floorboards under each of their feet. My grandmother died when my mother was still a young girl and, since then, only one thing in this room has ever changed. On the floor, at the side of the bed, there's an oval of darker wood where, until I was a thirteen, a rag rug was always placed just so. When I kneel down and touch the floor there, I remember how it was like so many other things that once belonged to my grandmother. For reasons I didn't understand, it was sacred.

One day the only cat my mother ever let me have became trapped in that bedroom and vomited on her precious rug. Rather than toss it out as a ruined bit of otherwise worthless nostalgia, or throw it in the wash with the rest of the rags, Mom carefully bathed it in the tub, easing away the crust of digestive fluid with my old baby brush.

By the time I came home from school my cat was gone. Mom had stuffed him in a cardboard box and driven to the farm, where my grandfather lived with my Great Aunt Gutherie, a sour spinster who made herself useful enough to stay.

An indoor cat that was used to predictable dinners, Socks was found dead a few weeks later, killed by a coyote that must've found him easier to get at than the chickens, which were kept safely shut inside their coop at night.

The last time I saw my mother alive was early last December. I drove all night, blowing snow making the usual two-hour trip from Regina a wheel-gripping four, until I finally pulled up in front of the house near midnight.

As always, my father had left the porch light on for me and was dozing in a living room chair when I let myself in. It was an old habit of his, waiting up for me. Mom couldn't go to sleep if she thought there might be a knock at the door in the middle of the night. With Dad keeping watch, if I didn't come home and was discovered lying in a ditch somewhere, he'd be the one to meet the police at the front door. He could break the bad news to Mom, gently, after breakfast.

"Hi, honey, rough trip?" Dad had yawned and stood up when I came in and shoved the front door shut hard against a gust of wind and snow and an ill-fitted frame. I stomped my boots, snow slagging away from them to melt on the rubber mat that filled the entryway.

"No worse than usual." We both knew it was a lie, the kind we always told if Mom was in the room. Even when she had still been lucid. "How is she?"

My mother had been diagnosed with dementia a year earlier and ever since we had watched her give in to it as though she were crawling under a warm blanket for a long and needed sleep.

"I think she's still awake. Why don't you go on up and check on her before you head in."

Abandoning my suitcase, I flapped my arms out of my winter parka and headed up the stairs, padding softly over the hallway floorboards without causing a noise.

"Mom?" I said quietly when I reached her half-opened door. I leaned in and found her sitting up in bed, an afghan and lamplight draped across her lap along with a picture album open to the middle. She was staring off into a corner of the room as though she truly was somewhere else. Off wandering through those pictures, perhaps. Re-imagining our history.

"Mom? It's me. I just got here." I stepped round to the side of the bed and knelt on the bare floor where that old rug used to be. When she didn't acknowledge me at first I rested my head on the mattress, tired from the trip, tired of pretending I didn't think dementia was just another way for her to keep me at a distance.

After a few minutes I lifted my head when my mother spoke.

"This was my daughter," she said. Her words came slowly and she paused, seeming to search for her next syllable. "Tess," she added with some difficulty and pointed to the page she'd stopped on. Both sides were covered in a tidy collage of pictures. Me as a grass-skirted hula girl in my first figure skating recital, dressed in stiff corduroy slacks and vest for my first day of the third grade. Another of me hugging Socks.

"Mom, that's me," I said and covered the papery skin of her cool, age-mottled hands with mine. Like everything else about her, her hands had aged suddenly, blotting out the woman she used to be.

"No," she said. "My daughter died a long time ago. Like everyone else."

I looked into my mother's face, expecting to find the worry creases she'd always worn at the corners of her eyes between her brows. They weren't there. Her face after all her years, was more peaceful than I'd ever seen. As though in believing she had really, finally, lost those she always pushed away — seeming to test whether we'd keep coming back — she had found a way to let go.

I took the album and closed it lightly, kissed my mother on the cheek, and turned out the lamp. When I went downstairs, Dad was waiting for me in the kitchen with a pot of camomile tea.

"Figured you probably drank a lot of coffee on the way here," he said and handed me a clunky mug, which I'd always preferred to Mom's dainty china teacups that had been passed down to her from my grandmother. Now, Mom is gone and I can hardly believe how distant that night seems. And I'm here, alone, following my mother's footsteps into her kitchen.

I open the door to her tea cupboard where delicate cups still dangle by their ears from small brass hooks. The hooks were installed because of the trains that sped along the tracks just yards from our back fence.

The whole house rattled when the trains passed by, carrying their heavy loads of wheat and potash out of the province, causing the china to tremble to the edge of their shelf. So I suppose it may have seemed deliberate when, a few days after my cat was eaten by coyotes, I opened the cabinet door and one of the teacups fell, breaking in half against the sharp edge of the countertop before tumbling to the floor and shattering.

My mother rushed into the kitchen, already wringing her hands. "What did you do?" She grasped my arm with anxious, pinching fingers that would leave a bruise.

"It — it fell," I said. "I didn't mean — It was just there when I opened the door. I tried to catch it." For proof I held out my hand, which had been cut against a falling shard.

"But you didn't catch it." She sucked in a thin, serrated breath before she let go of me and stared at the shelf, as though expecting to see the rest of her teacups lined up along the edge, ready to leap down after the first. Tenderly, nervously, she nudged each one to the back of the cupboard, counting as she touched their rims. With one gone, the remaining ones could no longer be called a set.

She knelt and, with shaking hands, began to pick up the pieces of broken pottery into her apron.

"From now on you don't touch these," she said. She glanced at the blood that was dripping slowly from my fingers. I thought she'd offer a Band-Aid, but she only cradled the broken cup in her lap, fitting a few pieces together as though it might miraculously be made whole again if it was all accounted for, and fault assigned.

"We could try to glue it," I said, tucking my hand behind me.

My mother was quiet for a moment. "And do what with it? Tea would dribble into my lap. It's in a hundred pieces. No. No it's broken, and that's that." She stood up, found a small box in a drawer, arranged the shards inside and placed the box on the shelf with the rest of the cups.

While I swept up what remained, dust and slivers, Mom went upstairs to lay a cold cloth over her eyes. She disappeared into her bedroom, drew the blinds and didn't come back downstairs until after I'd left for school the next morning. By then my father had installed the hooks.

My mother's name was Penelope Reimer. Her own mother, Ada, was not like those of her friends.

Ada was raised in the city — Winnipeg, an entire province away — and wasn't the sort of woman who could be kept cheerful with the daily busyness that would be hers as the wife of a farmer. After she married Joseph, she seemed to think that anything lacking in the way of society and culture would be made up for in views and experiences to fill her journals and watercolours.

By the time Penelope was about to go into the seventh grade at the country school near their farm, she had known for some years that Ada was becoming increasingly unhappy. When grownups didn't think Penelope could hear them they whispered things like, "That poor woman is like china in a bull shop. Never should've left the city." They shook their heads and *tsk*ed and prayed for her. Because of their own hardships, however, they were of the opinion that miracles were the exception, and suffering the better evidence of God's love.

As long as Penelope could remember, sadness seemed to come over Ada the way dark clouds stalked the horizon before closing in quickly and completely. Recently there was less and less space between those times. Hardly enough for them to get ready for the next storm.

Ada also suffered from headaches, which meant all the drapes in the house had to be drawn. And Penelope, who wasn't trusted not to carelessly make noise, was sent outside to amuse herself with whatever could be found lying around in the yard. Penelope though, who had gradually taken over Ada's share of inside chores while Joseph picked up the slack in the barn, had forgotten how to play. Her dollhouse was nothing more to her than a plywood box, emptied of the magic that once brought dolls to life.

Penelope spent weeks planting and tending her own little garden on the exposed side of the house, from a jar of miscellaneous seeds that turned out to have no practical use. She was secretly pleased when flowers grew up in the place of the expected carrots and kohlrabi and began to bud, until a windstorm came through and carried off the soil around them, exposing their roots.

In the evenings, when Penelope and Joseph returned to the house, she opened the front door and listened before going in.

Sometimes, Ada might be recovered and at the stove, humming while sprinkling spices into stew, eager for company. Other times, she was still in her nightgown, dishevelled and overwhelmed by the ingredients in front of her. On those days Penelope would quickly take over in the kitchen, but the simplest things would still pluck at the taut strings of Ada nerves. The sound of toast popping up was enough to make her startle, so that Penelope and her father developed a knack for quietly lifting the toaster's lever just when the bread was medium-browned. Between the two of them they almost always got there in time.

Penelope tried to think of other ways to help Ada. When one of her friends invited her to see a new litter of kittens, she told them she was busy, so she wouldn't be far should Ada call for her. She also tied lengths of cotton string from a leaky faucet to the drain, so drips would find a quiet way to the bottom of the sink. She made up the beds with fresh sheets on Saturday mornings, careful to run her hand along the entire grid of her mother's linens to make sure there was nothing to make her itch, no bits of hay that made their way through the wash to irritate her skin and scratch their way into her dreams. But no matter how Penelope tried to insulate Ada, her mother's nerves crackled with tension, like naked wires.

Finally, Joseph decided something had to be done.

"I've bought a house in town for you and your mother," he told Penelope one morning as the two of them sat at the kitchen table, eating bowls of cereal quietly. "She'll be happier. You'll go to a new school come fall and I'll visit on Sundays."

Penelope stared into her cereal. She thought about how, without her father there, there'd be no one to help remember the toast.

Penelope never wrote in her diary about how she felt. Just that moving to Swift Current, where there were shops and parks, revived Ada for a while. Even though the house was modest, bordered the railway, and had a summer kitchen for a back porch, she was cheered by the sight of people strolling along the sidewalks. Walking for the sake of walking, she said. Because there's more to life than work.

For a full month, and another after school started, Penelope and Ada kept busy cleaning, boarding up mouse holes, choosing wallpaper and fabrics, arranging the wedding dishes and tea set — which were too fine for the farm — in the kitchen cupboards. In the afternoons when Penelope returned from school, they started a new tradition. They had tea together, with cubes of white sugar dissolved in the bottom of their finely-painted china teacups.

"How was school today?" Ada would ask. "Did you make friends?"

"A few," Penelope would lie, anxious to keep her mother from knowing she sat alone at lunchtime, looking out the classroom window to avoid the other girls. It wasn't their fault. They had tried to be friendly. During her first week they included her in their secrets at recess, giggling at their own silliness. One morning though, Penelope was distracted by the thought that she'd left the stove lit after cooking cream of wheat. And although she tried, she couldn't make herself giggle along with the other girls. She stood as conspicuous as a hat rack while they gradually turned away.

Since then she'd watched them from a way off, wishing she could think of a reason to go over and talk to them again.

"You know Penelope, to make friends, you have to be a friend," Ada said, perhaps filling in what Penelope wasn't saying. Perhaps just filling in the silence. "Why don't you invite some girls over tomorrow? The house is ready for guests, don't you think? We'll have tea and biscuits." She looked around, seeming pleased with what she saw. Penelope thought she saw something else though, a familiar darkness that passed like a shadow over her mother's face.

"I don't think — " Penelope said, but stopped short of saying it wasn't a good idea. "Okay, I'll ask."

The next afternoon Penelope walked home with two other girls. Susan and Annabelle were "spirit sisters," they said, although they were as unrelated as pigs and pigeons. They dressed the same for school each day and braided each other's hair with wildflowers and dandelions. Penelope's promise of store-bought cookies, when all they'd ever had was homemade, was more than enough to tempt them. But when she led them up the porch steps and opened the front door, she knew by the tightly-closed drapes that Ada was having one of her spells.

Still on the porch, Penelope closed the door and backed up so quickly that she bumped into Susan and Annabelle. The two were holding hands as though they were Siamese twins joined at the palms.

"Hey," they said in one voice, stumbling, but not letting go of one another.

"Sorry." Penelope grasped the doorknob again, trying to think of a reason to go back to school. In the end there was no way out. With a deep breath, she pushed the door open and led the girls inside.

"So, do you live here alone or something?" Susan said loudly as Annabelle went to part the heavy living room curtains. Sharp angles of afternoon light fell across the floor. Neither of them noticed a mouse hunkered down in the middle of the living room. It had helped itself to a dish of stale marshmallow peanuts on the coffee table, but must have frozen when the three girls came inside.

"I think my mom is sleeping," Penelope said in a near whisper meant as a hush. She was anxious about upsetting Ada. Nearly as much though, she worried that Ada might come downstairs, nightgowned and agitated, and embarrass her in front of Susan and Annabelle.

Penelope made tea, catching the kettle before it whistled. She arranged cinnamon biscuits on an everyday plate, poured milk into a cream jug and set out a bowl of sugar cubes, along with three teacups that no one cared about. Before she could ask Susan and Annabelle whether they preferred lemon and honey, she heard a thump from upstairs, followed by the sound of Ada's voice crying out.

Penelope's heart became a stone in her chest. As calmly as she could, she set down the biscuit box and arranged her face into an apology, then quickly turned to leave the room, her legs as wobbly as cooked noodles.

"You might need help," Susan said. Both girls stood to follow Penelope, eager as volunteers to clean up after a church bake sale.

"No, it's fine," Penelope said, but Susan and Annabelle were like burrs on her socks. They stuck right on her heels and Penelope was too flustered to pick them off. "Okay, just wait here," she said with as much authority as she could when they reached Ada's room at the top of the stairs.

Penelope found her mother bent over her knees on the rag rug beside her bed, a stream of thin, white-flecked vomit spooling out in front of her. On the nightstand were an empty pitcher of water and a tipped-over bottle of Aspirin, the last few tablets spilled out.

"Did you take all these?" Penelope said, trying to keep panic from rising into her voice. She stepped round her mother and knelt next to her.

"Just a few at first," Ada said, looking up and reaching a cold and trembling hand for Penelope's. "For my head. I had to do something, but they didn't help so I took more." She turned her face away, rested her forehead back on her knees and quietly began to sob. "I thought I was better."

"Tell me what I should do," Penelope said, wiping at tears that sprung onto her cheeks. Her mother said nothing.

When Penelope left Ada's room to fetch a cold cloth for her face, she found Susan nervously chewing her thumbnail. Annabelle had disappeared.

"She went for her mom," Susan said. "We didn't know what else to do."

Penelope took a deep breath, went into the bathroom and turned on the tap.

Moments later, Annabelle and her mother were followed into the house by a man whom Penelope mistakenly thought must be Annabelle's father.

"She's fine," Penelope said, coming halfway down the stairs and standing in their way. "She's in her nightgown. She won't want company right now."

"I think I'll have to be the judge of that," the man said, introducing himself as Doctor Westfall. He put out his hand as if to greet Penelope, but when by habit she extended hers, he relieved her of the cloth she was holding and made his way past her, shutting her attempts to follow him into her mother's bedroom.

"Come, dear," said Annabelle's mother. "My daughter tells me that you made some tea. Why don't we go downstairs and enjoy it before it's hopelessly cold?"

Without thinking, Penelope obeyed. She watched dimly as the woman sent the other girls home, shushing their protests that they should be allowed to stay.

For what seemed like hours, Penelope sat at the kitchen table while Annabelle's mother busied herself with the few dishes in the sink. She swept the floor before starting a pot of soup.

Penelope absently accepted tea and a plate of toast with butter and cheese spread. Slowly she began to settle down. She closed her eyes and took deep breaths.

Some time later, Doctor Westfall came downstairs into the kitchen.

"She purged the Aspirin and I've given her some pills to help with sleep. It's enough for now, but I've also written a script for more." He looked around, as though unsure to whom he should give the prescription. Finally he settled on Penelope, but Annabelle's mother quickly stepped forward and took the paper from him.

"Thank you, Doctor," she said. "I'll take care of things here until arrangements are made."

That evening Penelope's father drove into town, but it was Annabelle's mother who spent the night, and the next three after that. And although she knew better, Penelope began to hope she would never leave.

One afternoon, Penelope's Aunt Gutherie, Ada's oldest unmarried sister, arrived on the train from Winnipeg to take over.

With an enormous carpetbag and hair wound so tightly into a bun that it made her face look as though it was being tightened by a screw at the back of her head, Penelope could already tell that Aunt Gutherie didn't have a bone of nonsense in her whole being.

"Your mother needs quiet. Lots of quiet," she said once she assessed the situation. Already she'd found and flicked two mice out the front door with a straw broom and installed poison in all the places they might be likely to come back. Now she bobbled her head disapprovingly, causing a generous pinch of wattle under her chin to jiggle with authority. "That father of yours ought to have known better. Thinking he could bring a woman like my sister into the wilds and turn her into a milk maid. Well. It's a good thing I've come is all I can say."

Within hours of Aunt Gutherie's arriving, a curtain of silence was pulled around the house, quarantining them from the rest of the neighbourhood. Inside, the atmosphere was like a funeral home. Voices were hushed and clutter forbidden, with Penelope sent to her room except when she was needed, or when Ada called for her.

"Don't go tiring her out," Aunt Gutherie said before she'd give Penelope permission to enter her mother's room. So Penelope sat mouse-like on the corner of the bed and quietly worried the plain hem of her school dress, stopping only long enough to answer her mother's questions. When she fell asleep, Penelope crept slowly, noiselessly, out of the room.

Under Aunt Gutherie's care, Ada began to improve. Not suddenly, as when they first moved into town. This time it was gradual until, after several weeks, she even began to wait for Penelope on their front porch after school, standing and waving when she saw her coming up the block. Together they'd go inside and share a pot of tea while Aunt Gutherie hovered nearby.

Some days Penelope's father would drop by with sacks of flour and sugar, and boxes of fresh fruit, then leave, saying the cows'd soon need to be milked. At the door, Joseph would pull a nickel from behind Penelope's ear. And then he'd be gone for another week.

One Friday, as Penelope was on her way home from school, she saw Ada as usual, standing on the porch, and when she got closer, there was Joseph too, on hands and knees, removing successful mouse traps from under the porch. His overalled legs and manure-encrusted barn boots stuck out from under the structure like half of a scarecrow. At irregular intervals, he flung traps, still clamped around dead mice, onto the grass at his side.

"Hey, there," he said when he finally emerged and saw Penelope.

"Hi," she said, looking over his shoulder to her mother.

"Seems you ladies have a few more mice than you need." He chuckled, a sound like pebbles tumbling, and turned his attention back to the traps. Levering the springs to release the dead mice into a bucket, he smeared fresh daubs of peanut butter on the mechanisms and crawled back under the porch.

"There," Joseph said when the job was done. "That ought to do you for a little while, don't you think?"

"Probably not," Penelope said. "It would be better to have a cat around. We have more mice than you do at home on the farm." She walked up the front steps and left the door open for her mother to follow her inside. A little later she realized her father had left without saying goodbye. Later that evening, after Ada had gone to her room for the night, he returned carrying a box with holes punched into the sides. Aunt Gutherie met him at the door.

"Brought a little something to help out with your mouse problem," he said. He held the box high and peered over top of the woman until he saw Penelope standing in the kitchen door, wiping her hands on a dish towel. "It was your idea," he said to Penelope, taking half a step inside. Aunt Gutherie held her ground, but Joseph was a large man and pushed forward until he'd gained his way inside.

Penelope could smell fresh hay, and there were sounds coming from inside the box. Scratching and mewling. She felt her whole face stretch into a smile.

"No. Absolutely not. There will be no animals in my house," Aunt Gutherie said, folding her arms across her chest.

Penelope's expression collapsed.

"But this is not your house," Joseph said. He carefully opened the box flaps to reveal a mother cat, blinking against the lamplight, and four kittens. He bent down to set them on the floor.

"Are they going to live here?" Penelope said, already kneeling next to the box as the mother cat began to bathe the bottom of a kitten who, although his eyes were still glued shut, was more intent on exploring the inside of the box than getting cleaned.

"The big one can live outside and take care of the mice. But those little ones have to go back. Tonight."

"Gutherie," Joseph said. "These kittens are too young to be separated from their mother. Surely you can see they'll have to stay with her."

"There's no reason on God's earth to keep them. You're a farming man. Don't tell me you don't know how to deal with an unwanted brood."

Penelope felt heat flood her chest like hot wax that spread through her whole body until her legs felt weak like a warm candle. She knew what sometimes had to be done when there were too many kittens on the farm.

"No, you can't!" she cried and leaned protectively over the box, wrapping her arms around its sides. She could hear the mother cat purring as she flopped onto her side and, one by one, the kittens began to nurse, paddling against her loose belly with their tiny, flat paws.

Aunt Gutherie was quiet for a moment. She had only one move left.

"Think of your poor wife. Her nerves can't take this kind of shock."

Penelope could feel her father backing down. He stood up straight but his hands disappeared into his pockets.

"Fine," he said. "Let my wife decide what to do with them. Until then Penelope can have them for company. They won't be a bother to anyone for a night or two."

"Just take them back," Penelope said. "We can get more traps for the mice. I can empty them out."

"I have too many cats already," Joseph said. "Now be a good girl and listen to what your mother decides."

"Oh, for crying out loud," Aunt Gutherie said. "They're just animals. There's more where those ones came from."

Penelope wanted to say that there were plenty of people too, and more where they came from. But she knew it wasn't the same thing.

All that night Penelope guarded those kittens from Aunt Gutherie, who hovered like a buzzard in a lace collar.

When the mother cat needed to be let out to "violate the flower beds", Aunt Gutherie gave it a not-quite-mean shove with the side of her shoe and closed the door tightly behind it. She seemed satisfied to have gotten rid of at least one of them. When the cat came back and scratched at the door half an hour later, Penelope scooped it up along with the kittens and carried them all up to her room, pushing a dresser in front of the door to keep Aunt Gutherie out.

The next morning Penelope found her aunt and mother sitting at the kitchen table. The sound of the kettle nearing a boil came from the kitchen.

"Did she tell you what Dad said?" Penelope said, crossing her arms.

"I told her it won't do any good letting you get attached when we each of us know full well they can't stay," Aunt Gutherie said. She stood up and lifted the kettle from the stove. "Soon those cats'll be full-grown toms, out doing their filthy business, caterwauling at all hours and messing in the neighbours' yards."

Penelope was prepared to argue, but Ada patted her arm and said, "They're just little kittens. Harmless. Penelope will take care of them and they won't be any bother."

"And who'll look after them while the girl's in school?" Aunt Gutherie said. "No. It's unfortunate, but they have to go." A moment later, she set down a cup of camomile tea for Ada. The tea, if it wasn't needed at the moment to calm Ada, was always a good way to remind her that she could have a nervous episode any time.

Ada's hand trembled a little as she lifted the cup, a splash of tea spilling over the side.

"Before long those ones will grow up and be after each other and we'll be overrun with inbreds," Aunt Gutherie said. "It's a mercy to do away with a few now instead of a few dozen later. Now, Penelope, go on up and get them. No sense putting it off." Penelope looked to her mother, but Ada was a fly caught in honey. Or vinegar.

Penelope went upstairs as she was told. But instead of delivering the kittens to her aunt she crept past the living room and into the kitchen. A few more steps, avoiding well-known creaks in the floor, and she was at the back door and into the porch-like summer kitchen that held a stove for canning and a small fridge that was kept unplugged and propped open to keep it from smelling. Penelope let the mother cat outside and turned her attention to the kittens.

Even though they'd never even turned on the oven to see whether it worked, Penelope couldn't bring herself to hide the kittens in there. It brought to mind too terrible a possibility. When she finally decided where to hide them she went outside and waited, hiding around the corner when her aunt stuck out her head and called.

After a long while, when Penelope returned without the kittens, Ada was sitting alone at the kitchen table, her hands folded calmly around a teacup.

"Maybe we can find homes for them when they're a little older," she said. "What do you think? Might a few of your friends like to each take one?"

Penelope bit her lips in confusion. She had been sure Ada would agree with Aunt Gutherie.

"Really?" she said, twisting her fingers together. "I could keep them until then?"

"Of course you can," Ada said, the dark blue of her eyes bright under a film of tears. She reached out and held Penelope's hands so lightly it was like being held by a pair of empty silk gloves. "I know you didn't want to move away from the farm. The least I can do is let you have a little bit of it here for a while." She held out her arms, and Penelope was drawn by them until she was almost sitting on Ada's lap.

"My poor Nella Pea," her mother said. "You've had to be so strong, haven't you?"

After a few moments Penelope moved to the chair next to Ada, who pushed a teacup towards her. Together they sat in silence, sipping tea and sniffling from time to time.

"I hid the kittens," Penelope finally said, laughing a little, wiping her nose on the back of her hand, even though she knew it was a disgusting thing to do. "I thought Aunt Gutherie would have a fit when I didn't come back right away."

"Well, she did. But let's not think of that. Come, why don't you introduce me to those kittens of yours."

Together Penelope and Ada went out to the porch, hand in hand. Penelope felt like a bottle of soda pop that would let out all its bubbles if opened. She wanted to hold in the feeling forever. But when she led her mother to the fridge where she'd hidden the kittens, closing it tight to keep their cries from giving them away, she felt Ada's hand go slack. Penelope looked up to see that her mother's face had become ashy.

"Oh, no, Penelope. Tell me they're not in there. There's not enough air," She closed her eyes and withdrew her hand.

"I–I wanted to hide them from Aunt. I just. What's wrong? What did I do?" Penelope clasped her hands over her throat before she swung around and tugged open the fridge door. "They're fine. Look. They're asleep."

When Penelope reached for one of the kittens though, it was limp like a tiny pair of pyjamas.

Sound seeped from Penelope's mouth like air from a balloon. "Oh, no." She knelt and her hands shook as she checked each kitten until she found one that was still alive, but barely. Penelope drew it to her chest and lowered her head. She turned to her mother, but Ada was already going back inside the house, calling for Aunt Gutherie.

In a moment Aunt Gutherie was there to help Ada away, leaving Penelope kneeling on the floor, cradling the nearly dead kitten. The mother cat, when she pawed her way back through the unlatched porch door, would no longer accept it.

For the next two days, every few hours, while Ada closed herself in her room, Penelope nursed the kitten, filling up an eyedropper from a bowl of warm milk, painstakingly squeezing a drop at a time into its mouth. Even though it seemed at first to recover a little, soon it could no longer keep the milk down. It aspirated more than it swallowed and vomited tiny puddles of curdled liquid into Penelope's hands until it finally died.

When Penelope went to Ada's room to tell her, she was sent out of the room by her aunt.

Over the next weeks, things began to return to the way they were before the kittens. Ada got out of bed and was ready to meet Penelope at the front door after school. But Penelope knew something unnameable had shifted. When they went inside for tea, Ada's expression was thin and brittle. She held onto a fragile china cup, cradling it with two hands as though it was an eggshell.

It's hard to tell from Penelope's diary exactly how much time passed between what happened with the kittens and when Ada took her own life.

One day Penelope was walking home from school. A block away she stopped to pick a few stems of lilacs, their hundreds of purple blossoms still tightly closed like tiny fists. She'd had to twist their supple green branches from the overgrown bush on the corner of Spinster Shellenberg's yard, keeping out of sight so she wouldn't get caught and scolded away with a broom.

Lilacs were Ada's favourite flower, so Penelope twisted the stems until they were free and her hands were sticky with lilac sap. When she lifted the blossoms to her nose she breathed in their sweet, cool perfume, feeling her posture straighten like a cut stem put into water. She walked, skipped a little, the hem of her dress a pale-yellow bell around her knees.

Within sight of the house Penelope began to run, the wands of lilacs held out to her sides, trailing scent. As she came to the exact square of sidewalk where she could suddenly see her own front door, she stumbled to a stop. The lilacs fell from her fingers, their dense clusters bouncing apart into separate stems beside her feet. Instead of Ada, Aunt Gutherie was on the front steps, wringing her hands together and looking down the street towards Penelope.

Penelope felt her breath being forced out of her as though she'd suddenly been squeezed. She wanted to take off in both directions at once, but found she could only move forward.

"The doctor's on his way. There's no need to go up there," Aunt Gutherie said, trying to block Penelope from going inside. She was visibly shaken by whatever had happened, and a poor guard. Penelope pushed past her as though she were a heavy curtain and came to stand at the bottom of the stairs.

Penelope was out of breath, but not from running. Now that she was here, she didn't want to go up. Slowly though, she began to climb the stairs. When she reached her mother's room, the cold weight of the doorknob filled her hand. The door seemed heavier than she remembered. Its bottom edge pushed over the carpet with a hush, as though telling her to keep quiet.

Without making a sound, Penelope went in and knelt down next to Ada's body. She'd fallen from the bed onto the rag rug she insisted on saving to stop the chill from seeping through the floor.

A froth of red-streaked saliva, from the sleeping pills Penelope would learn her mother had swallowed, was smeared across her cheek.

"For Godsakes, child," Aunt Gutherie said, her voice shrill and obscene, like laughter in church.

"Leave us alone," Penelope said, stroking Ada's damp hair, stringy with sweat. "She doesn't need you anymore."

"She needed someone a half hour ago is what. In fact, she needed someone to stop her from running off to this province in the first place. It's what killed her, as surely as I know anything. She should've stayed home."

Still, Penelope refused to move until the doctor came.

"I thought I told you to keep the child out of here," he said, looking at Aunt Gutherie as though she was as stupid a woman as he'd ever met. He made a short irritated sound. "I don't suppose you can tell me when the husband might arrive."

"No, well, you were the only person I thought to call," she said, stammering. It was the first time Penelope had ever seen her aunt cowed by anyone.

"Go down and call him this minute." To Penelope he said, "Come away, now. It's time to let me take care of her. You go with your aunt and wait for your father. It shouldn't take him more than twenty minutes, don't you think?"

Penelope waited at the bottom of the stairs for the doctor to come back down.

Penelope stopped writing in her journal after Ada's funeral. But the rest is what I've always known.

Aunt Gutherie raised Penelope until she was old enough to marry. A short time after that, she and my father had me. And except for the two things I destroyed, Ada's teacup and, later, her rag rug, the house stayed exactly as it was since the time of Ada's death.

Not long after the rug incident, the day I learned that Socks had been killed out on the farm, my mother met me at the front door after school and tried to say she was sorry. I wouldn't hear her.

"It's your fault. It's all your fault!" I ran into the house and up the stairs, into her bedroom. I snatched the rug my cat had soiled, the rug Ada had died on, and stomped back down and out of the house into the backyard. I climbed the fence and as a train approached, threw the rug onto the track.

"What have you done?" My mother was stiff with anger when she found me, having discovered what I'd taken. The train was still clamouring past, car after car.

"I don't know what you're talking about."

"You know very well what I mean."

I looked over my shoulder at the train before turning back to face her, daring her to yell at me, tell me she cared more about the rug than she did about me.

"You probably wish I'd thrown myself on the tracks instead, don't you?"

My mother lifted her hand as though she was about to slap me. In one movement though, she lowered her hand and closed the space between us, wrapped me up in her arms. When I tried to pull away, she only held on tighter.

Acknowledgements:

These stories would not exist without my husband, who never asked how much longer it was going to take, nor once brought up the "job" word.

I owe my sister, co-heir to whatever truth is in the fiction, credit for at least a few of my favourite lines. Thank you so much for getting on that October bus.

Sandra Birdsell was my writing instructor through The Humber School for Writers mentorship program. I am grateful to her for expectations so high that I forgot to rinse the conditioner out of my hair.

My writing posse from Humber helped me tread water while always insisting land was in sight. Among them, particular thanks go to Susan Toy, for reading and critiquing early drafts, wedging open doors and pushing me through them. And Vicky Bell, who gave considerable editing advice and asked nothing in return.

Elsie K. Neufeld, editor of *Half In The Sun: Anthology of Mennonite Writers*, opened an early door and has never closed it.

Thank you to Thistledown for rejecting these stories five years ago, and Antanas Sileka, Director of the Humber School for Writers, for providing such a rare proving ground. To Margaret Hart, my agent from the Humber School for Writers Literary Agency, for saving me from myself more than once. And my amazing editor, Susan Musgrave, for culling commas and not holding back.

Thank you to my Grandma and Grandpa Friesen, for all the love and *varenyky*. To Nancy Tordiffe, for prayers that moved mountains.

And while I hope to never again hear the words, "Why don't you send your stories to Oprah?" I thank my mother for her unswerving belief that Oprah would have called.

Darcie Friesen Hossack is a graduate of the Humber School for Writers. She has been a food writer for the *Kelowna Daily Courier* and *Kamloops This Week* for the past six years, and most recently, thepeartree. ca. Her story "Little Lamb" was nominated for the 2008 McClelland & Stewart Journey Prize.

CPSIA information can be obtained at www.ICGtesting.com
Printed in the USA
LVOW080842211011

251416LV00003B/2/P